First published in Great Britain in 2008 by Comma Press
www.commapress.co.uk

First published in Barcelona as *T'estimo si he begut* by Acantilado: Quaderns Crema
S.A, 2004.

A CIP catalogue record of this book is available from the British Library.

ISBN   1905583176
ISBN-13   978 1905583171

With the support of the Culture Programme (2007-2013) of the European Union.

Education and Culture DG

Culture Programme

Culture

This project has been funded with support from the European Commission.
This publication reflects the views only of the author, and the Commission
cannot be held responsible for any use which may be made of the information
contained therein.

The publisher gratefully acknowledges assistance from the Arts Council England
North West.
Set in Bembo 11/13 by David Eckersall
Printed and bound in England by SRP Ltd, Exeter

I Love You When I'm Drunk

by
Empar Moliner

Translated from the Catalan by
Peter Bush

Contents

The Invention of Aspirin

Eighteen minutes into dinner at the Mexican restaurant and Mrs Salat is so bored out of her mind she decides to do a couple of things to ensure she survives the time remaining: she will sink one margarita after another and imagine her husband isn't her husband. From now on Mr Crespí is her husband and not Mr Salat. She likes Mr Crespí. He's not her hubby.

The passage of time becomes more bearable. After each margarita, she feels more optimistic and by number twenty the earth is one big soft cheese, Mr Crespí is her husband, hangovers never were and Mr Salat ceases to annoy. From now on, Mr Salat is Mrs Crespí's husband, and she no longer has to feel responsible for what he says or does. Or be embarrassed he gets so petulant when tasting the wine (he ordered wine). She couldn't care less if he takes ages to finish his food because he likes to rabbit on so. Or soils his napkin or asks the waiter what's in each dish, even the guacamole, and whether it's very piquant. Or is always saying he's got another story to tell. Or if he says: 'I shall now tell you all something you will find hugely amusing.' She's now Crespí's wife, and he behaves perfectly. She imagines how she and Crespí will go home after the dinner. They'll go to bed. He'll strip off without more ado and grab the box of condoms – maybe after asking where it is. She looks forward to the moment he'll roll it on. She knows, from Mrs Crespí, that he's always in the mood.

When they bid farewell, she concludes, happily, that she's not been half as bored as she usually is, and that nobody gets drunk on margaritas. The two men shake hands energetically and say they must do this more often. The women kiss on the cheek and promise it won't be so long to the next time the foursome dines out. But Crespí puts his arm round her shoulder and doesn't bid farewell. Mr Salat, her husband, is the one to bid farewell. He gives her a peck on each cheek as if she weren't his wife.

'Shall we be off?' asks Mr Crespí.

And as a taxi is already drawing up, he opens the door and in she goes, quite terrified. Perhaps she's a little tipsy but it hasn't gone to her head yet. Or perhaps the other three are having fun at her expense. She sits down and lets Crespí indicate their destination. The taxi-driver signals, moves into the right-hand lane, and advances slowly towards the red traffic light ahead. It's not cold and nothing looks any different. In a cash dispenser foyer a group of Pakistani flower sellers are crouching in prayer. Their faces turn to the show adverts; their bums point to the cash machine. They've put their flowers on the ground.

'The Salats are so tiresome,' Mr Crespí complains. 'He's appalling. Did you see how he kept stirring his wine?'

'Yes,' mutters Mrs Salat.

No doubt about it. She *is* his wife now.

She knows the Crespí's place, but not like her own home. She's never been inside the couple's bedroom, only seen it from the outside, but she doesn't make a single wrong move. She undresses and puts her things in the right place. She gets into bed and knows which side is hers. Mr Crespí comes right away and also gets undressed. He scratches his testicles and sniffs his armpits. (Mrs Crespí had complained to her endlessly about this behaviour.)

Once he's in bed, she climbs on top of him and nibbles his ear. She's so hungry for it! She's not thought of anything else the whole night. He gets an immediate hard on and grabs her tits. She yelps, taken aback.

When they finish, he's almost in tears. He confesses he's

not known her so up for it in years. That she's acted like a nymphomaniac (words of praise in his book). Indeed, until now he'd always thought she was frigid.

'I'm ovulating,' she apologises. And kisses him on his Adam's apple. She picks up the book on the night table, the one Mrs Crespí was reading, and opens it up at the right page. She instantly recalls the plot.

In the morning she puts on the apple-green knickers and bra she finds in a drawer. She selects a tartan skirt and white blouse. Then has a re-think.

Hell! She'll put on that designer dress, the one Mrs Crespí keeps for grand occasions. The face-creams she finds in the bathroom are also more expensive than hers, and she decides to apply them generously. And she likes the job she has now a lot more. As Mrs Salat, she worked in a mobile phone shop. Now, in her new skin, she's a secretary in a market-research firm.

Neither the porter nor colleagues on her floor look surprised to see her. They sing the praises of her dress. She's Mr Crespí's wife, in everyone's eyes, and perhaps will be forever. As she speaks to people, she remembers her name, life-story and whether she feels well or not.

At lunchtime she avoids the colleagues who ask if she wants to go to the café to have a fat-free diet snack. She takes a taxi to the mobile phone shop. She watches the real Mrs Crespí through the shop-window. She's wearing her denim shirt, the one they bought together, the one she'd always found very fetching. It doesn't look bad on her. She's also snaffled her black Lycra bra. But not the knickers, they were in the wash. She attends to an old couple. She watches her use a thumbnail to unstick a piece of sellotape from a hands-free kit. She doesn't think she's got up to anything with Mr Salat. He's not the kind who thinks about sex all day. You must be joking.

In the afternoon, she chairs a meeting with the head of marketing and three clients in the projection-room. They are studying a survey on trends in the consumption of chewing gum and dim the light so they can see the screen properly. Their clients aren't at all sure how to focus their campaign and the head of marketing lists all the arguments. While he's speaking, Mrs Salat gives him a good look over: his hair is crinkly and his long, sharp canines give him a rather bee-like face. Her thoughts go on the rampage. She tries a repeat of what she did the previous night: she imagines the head of marketing is her lover. Whenever the head of marketing addresses her, she looks normal and aloof so their clients don't rumble her.

At the end of the meeting, he calls her into his office. Mrs Salat picks up her folder, pens and bag. She knocks on the door.

'Come in.'

Once inside, the head of marketing shuts the door and throws himself at her. Mauls and slaps her.

'You got me panting for it in the meeting, you sex-pot!'

'I'm all wet, you idiot!' she responds. And also clouts him one. He grips her by the neck as if to strangle her. She sticks her knee in his testicles. They fight.

'Get your knickers down or I'll kill you!' he whispers.

And she obeys. She knows the head of marketing's next step will be to open his filing cabinet and take out ropes and a tube of Vaseline. To save time, she sits on his ergonomic chair; a chair with a purple seat and no backrest.

'I'll muzzle you so you don't start to shout, you dirty...' he warns her, as he covers her mouth with sticking plaster.

'Ohh!' she sighs.

The head of marketing unzips his trousers. He says he wants her stark naked in the middle of his office. He stands behind her and lifts up her dress. They breathe heavily. He tells her he wants her to go downstairs and do it with the porter. With the porters, rather. He wants to involve more than one. The porters from every shift. One after another. Or two at a time.

When they finish, he eases her lovingly away from his body.

'I love you...' he whispers, on his knees, cradling her sore wrists. 'I can't live without you.'

'Leave your wife and I'll believe you,' she answers, still heaving. And she cleans herself with two intimate hygiene wipes she's just remembered she always keeps in her handbag.

He huffs, bored. Buttons up. He can't leave her, he's told her a thousand times. He can't do a thing like that to Berta. (Berta, she intuits, is the head of marketing's adolescent daughter.) Why can't they just stay as they are. Aren't they having a good time? She looks down and mumbles that she doesn't know how he can be so weak-minded. But she understands now. And to show him she understands, she'd just decided she wants to meet his wife. She wants to go to dinner at his place with Mr Crespí. A dinner party for the two couples.

'And you'll get me all hot and bothered again, you hairy little pussy?' his voice had perked up again. 'But no knickers, it's a deal?'

'Tonight, right.'

As she leaves his office tidying her dress, she avoids the backwards glance of a female colleague, who immediately averts her gaze and behaves as if she's working on her computer. They must all be in the know about her fling with the head of marketing. She picks the phone up and as soon as her finger touches the keypad she remembers Crespí's mobile number. She greets him with the news of their dinner-date for that night.

During the meal, Mrs Salat imagines, rather more routinely, that the head of marketing is her husband. As she'd already anticipated, the head of marketing's wife leaves with Mr Crespí and she stays at home with the head of marketing and his adolescent daughter. She's amused to reflect that she's now the wife of the man who a few hours ago couldn't abandon his wife for her. Perhaps she should hint that she knows he has a lover at work.

She says 'good night' to his daughter and goes up to the bedroom with her new husband. But however much she licks and slavers over the nape of his neck, he pushes her roughly away and starts reading. Mrs Salat guesses, too late, that they've not had sex for years. Like Mr Salat and her. What should she call Salat now? Her ex?

In the morning, the head of marketing goes to the office, and she stays at home in her dressing gown flicking through the newspaper. She's suddenly horrified by the thought her imagination will dry up and she'll be forced to stay with the head of marketing forever. At the end of the day that would be more excruciating than being Mr Crespí's wife. She goes to the beautician, to the supermarket and has coffee with her lady friends. She gets home early because the daughter is coming to do her homework with her boyfriend, and she doesn't want to leave them alone.

While the young ones get their afternoon snack ready, she busies herself in the kitchen, and doesn't lose sight of them. She watches them open the fridge, get the cheese out and make sandwiches with sliced white. Quite spontaneously she starts imagining the girl's boyfriend stark naked. She tries to chase that one from her head. It's not right to think such things about a minor. He can't be sixteen yet. He wears a spike through his tongue that makes it difficult for him to speak properly. His chin is like an apricot, his eyebrows like a little devil's and he's got a big nose. The boy puts his hand under his t-shirt, absentmindedly. There's a big scratch between his ribs and navel. Maybe he's never done it, at least not yet.

Mrs Salat opens the fridge and takes out the plastic container of salami. She also makes herself a sandwich, and eats it with relish. She looks at the boy and turns red. What would it be like doing it with him? she wonders. In a flash, the adolescent asks her if she wants to play on the computer.

'Mum, we're going to play on my computer,' says Mrs Salat. And it is the adolescent girl who smiles and chides her: 'But finish your homework first.'

They go upstairs. Once in the bedroom, Mrs Salat declares: 'I've given it another think. I do think I feel ready to do it.'

He gets excited. He stammers. Berta had told him he could forget about deflowering her until they were both eighteen. He embraces her so deliriously she's forced to grip him by the shoulders and beg him not to be so rough.

During the week, Mrs Salat goes to secondary school, eats fast food, visits her chatrooms, listens to music on her Walkman and beds her boyfriend three times a day. She now realises she can't imagine she's anyone in particular's boyfriend, because pupils in other years and her friends' boyfriends are always asking if they can come and do their homework at her house. At the sec – Mrs Salat says that now: sec – the latest is that Berta is 'an easy lay' and is getting to be red-hot at oral sex. Even her teachers see her differently.

When she's fed up with going to school every day and the unbalanced diet she's on, she decides she's had enough. One evening when she stays for dinner at her boyfriend's place, she begins to imagine she is his father's wife. Not because she fancies her boyfriend's father but because she feels like a change of scene. Her boyfriend's father immediately hassles her because she's not banked the garage-hand's money as she promised she would. She becomes her boyfriend's father's wife for a week. When she's had her fill, she's her boyfriend's father's brother's wife and, then, the wife of the press officer of a political party with whom they had dinner one night. The press officer and his wife – her, now – dine with the general secretary of the political party and, for a few days, she is *his* wife. She's also the president's wife, and spends a busy, busy month greeting the populace from balconies and

7

inaugurating exhibitions.

She's a rock singer's wife and then the wife of a writer she's always admired. As the writer has lots of lovers, she becomes each one in turn. Then, she's back as his wife again and goes through his pockets: she finds notes written by herself in the depths of his jacket. One day she sees a couple quarrelling in a bar – the man seems so sad and humiliated by the shouting that Mrs Salat is grief-stricken. 'How can a woman make this sweet man so sad?' she wonders. And begins to imagine going out with him. And when she occupies the place of the woman chiding him, she kisses him and treats him lovingly. He turns out to be an actor in porn films, and she – now his fiancée – is also into pornography and occasionally does striptease at private parties. She's the lead actress in *Hardcore Innocence, Parts One, Two and Three,* and decides to call it a day when one stag night where she's the girl who pops out of the cake, she falls in love with the bridegroom. He's the handsomest man Mrs Salat has ever seen. She begins to imagine she's his fiancée. The wedding is tomorrow.

During the religious ceremony she contemplates the father of her husband-to-be, her future brothers-in-law, all as handsome as her husband, the waiters and the men who have come to the party. To think that by just using her imagination, they could all be hers, bores her stiff. She's sure everyone possesses this ability of hers except that nobody has ever imagined what she imagines, because nobody has ever been as bored out of her mind as she is. Fact is, no man can resist her, whoever he might be. Truth is, she's tried to imagine she's the wife of the models advertising underpants on the hoardings in bus shelters and it hasn't worked for her. But it would be easy enough to track them down to a catwalk where they were parading, if she was really that keen. What an empty thought, that till the day she dies, any man in the world could be up for servicing her. Why *do* people rate sex so highly? This makes her go all weepy at the party, but

8

everyone thinks she's only being a tearful bride. In the evening, she gets into the limo with the man who is now her husband. They'll go to their hotel and he, the man who's respected her up until that very instant, will want to lay her. Just the thought of it is a real drag. She doesn't feel like it. Not today. She's got such a headache.

Getting Rid of Pests

My wife comes and tells me we've got an appointment tomorrow to see a marriage counsellor. I say, 'Why?' 'Because we're like brother and sister,' she says, 'or don't you reckon we're like brother and sister?'

She means we've not had sexual relations for some time. She threatens to leave me, if I don't go. I don't believe her, but pretend I do. She doesn't *really* want to have sex again. She just wants someone to say she's in the right. When we still had occasional sex, say every four or five months, we had more rows than we do now. We were both very half-hearted. And the night when sex was supposed to be on – we knew when it was on because in the morning I'd ask her and she didn't say no – we always scrapped before going to bed and in the end didn't do it. It wasn't on purpose. We shouted at each other in front of the boy. She's foul-mouthed when she gets angry. She snarls, 'I don't fucking feel like it,' and so on. But now it's a piece of cake. If we get angry, it's all over in a couple of minutes. We each take a book to bed with us, and she jokes about wanting to push me on the floor. I don't know if she masturbates on the side. I do, big-time. But then I did it big-time when we used to have intercourse.

The counsellor is Dr Guallar. Her consultancy is in an old flat in the Eixample, with views front and back. There are watercolours of couples holding hands in reception that look as if they were a present from an artist, a grateful patient. Another couple is waiting opposite. My wife has put lipstick on and sits with her legs tightly pressed together as if she's nervous or feels out of place. Her lips are very thin, and if she

11

uses lipstick it draws attention to the marks on her face left by old spots.

As it's our first visit, we have to explain what our problem is to the counsellor. My wife does this. She says, 'We don't have sex.' I think it's a phoney way to talk. She never used to say 'have sex'. That's what young people say. She explains that the flame's gone out, that women like the excitement of seduction. I've seen in the magazines that she buys and the books written by women – she likes reading books by women – I've seen it really riles them a lot when you use dental floss in front of them. Dental floss is no big deal. It probably means you cut your nails out of sight and don't scratch your backside. I never use dental floss, it makes me want to vomit. If you do use floss, at least it means you're clean. I mean they still love you. I mean there's still hope, but not as far as we're concerned. Then it's my turn. I don't know what to say. What can *I* say? The counsellor asks me if I remember the last squabble we had.

'No.'

'Yesterday we squabbled about the way you eat,' my wife interjects.

I'd forgotten. She's always nagging me for being greedy, because I can't bear food being left over. She tells the counsellor that the way I eat 'defeats her' ('defeats me,' she says). If we're eating asparagus and prawns, I try to grab all the prawns. If we're going for aperitifs with other couples, I'll grab the last three anchovies and wolf them down, and don't spare a thought for the people who've not had a look in. I've no self-control at all-you-can-eat buffets.

'I'm really concerned,' she complains (to inveigle the doctor over to her side; she never talks like this). In the end I say she always messes up our food. She'll buy things and then let their sell-by date pass and throw them out before she's even opened them. I find this deplorable and sometimes I retrieve them from the bin and eat them.

Before we went, I'd imagined the counsellor would ask

stuff about out sex life. Whether in the course of our life together my wife has ever taken the initiative (she never has). And what's her attitude when I do? (She lets me get on with it). But the doctor says it's clearly all part of a much bigger problem. Perhaps, by grabbing prawns and throwing food away we are sending each other different messages. My wife is already in tears and is crying no doubt because she's embarrassed I said she throws things away. The doctor says we should forget sex for the moment and that, as a first step, she wants us each to make a list of the vices and virtues we see in the other. We mustn't show them to each other. And must bring them on our next visit.

We don't argue at all in the first week, because we're embarrassed about the doctor finding out. I make sure I don't grab any prawns, and it just so happens she throws nothing away. By the second week, our throwings out and salvagings are back to normal. The third week she insists we make a list, but only of our partner's defects and virtues. I try not to be too frank so she doesn't get angry. By the fourth week she's spelling out a system we must adopt when communicating with each other. It involves writing letters saying what we've liked or disliked about the other throughout the day. We must use a kind of template. 'Dear so-and-so,' and then, 'I would like to tell you how I feel because then you can help me and we can talk things through quietly.' After that it goes on: 'I regret to say that:' followed by dotted lines for criticism and praise.

My wife falls into line enthusiastically; I'm embarrassed. I tread the floor in fear I'll find a letter in the corner of every room. She never leaves them in the same place. She's always liked writing: she says she's a writer *manquée*. She writes a personal diary she keeps on her computer (the password is the boy's name). I've paid a visit and it's boring. She talks about me, our quarrels or her dream life. And her worries about the boy, like whether he'll smoke joints when he's older. She rates the films she sees and the books she reads on a scale from nought to ten. She writes to a confidante called Júlia. It's a name she likes a lot. When we didn't know whether the kid would be a girl or a boy, she always said if it were a girl, she'd be Júlia. He's Roc (that's also a name she chose).

When we were courting, she'd write me letters full of moons and stars, rabbits or cakes. She wrote imitation Miró style, with her 'a's and her 'o's in heavy black ink. If I didn't read them immediately, she got depressed. Then our boy was born, and we weren't so concerned about one another.

I find notelets for me left on the washbasin mirror and the microwave and even inside the toilet lid. She'll write, for example: 'Make sure you shut me when you're finished!' as if the lid were speaking. I can't stick a note on the carton of milk to the effect that: 'My time's up at twelve tomorrow. Use me. Don't throw me away.' You must be a born optimist to leave a note in a place like this. I pick them up in case the boy sees them and says: 'Dad, what's this all about?' Kids blab at school. One day, his teacher told me with a big laugh that the boy had told her about a story I tell him at night. It's a story about a fairy who looks like a singer we like and shows her breasts when someone tells the truth.

I sometimes act as if I've not seen her notes, but she's relentless. The counsellor tells me yet again I've got to open up and that I too should be writing them, and not just my wife. I try at the office, but I never know what to write. Nothing about her gets on my nerves during the day because I can't see her. On Sunday I find five of her letters at home, all under the same heading.

I have to choose my holiday dates at work and, though I'm a manager and have the right to ask for the best month, I opt for September. I say I like working in August, Barcelona's almost empty, and besides my wife's got her holidays in

14

September. What I tell her, on the other hand, is that we drew lots and I lost. She immediately writes me a letter saying she's very sorry we won't be on holiday together and that she feels very upset, even though the company is to blame and not me. I ask her, please, take an apartment and take the boy too, because he could do with a bit of sun and sand.

'Do you realise?' she reproaches me. 'This is just the kind of thing you could write to me, if you made the effort, and I would think it was so wonderful.'

I make an online reservation and no more is said. We go to the counsellor for the last time before the holidays and she concludes this parenthesis in our relationship is very timely. We should make the most of the break, and think of it as if we were fiancés. We can then try to seduce each other again. When we're saying goodbye she tells us she's off to Greece with some friends, 'but no men'. My wife doesn't react, but I smile, because I guess that she's separating.

The last day of July I drive them to the apartment and we eat in an Italian restaurant. Neither finishes their pizza and I can't stop myself eating her leftovers. The fact is I was still hungry. I say I will take what's left for breakfast, and my wife huffs and puffs. She asks me to speak to the waiter while she goes to the toilet, otherwise she'll explode. Before we say our goodbyes – I'm working in the morning – she sticks a letter in my pocket and says that, if she can't find an Internet café, we can swap notes at the weekends when I pay them a visit. She adds: 'I wrote that before the 'pizza episode,' my lad, for if I'd known that…'

As back-up for August, we contract a temporary receptionist by the name of Dolors. We got her through a temping agency. As it's summer and the owners aren't around, we all wear polos and gaudy t-shirts. She sometimes wears a long dress, buttoned down the front from top to bottom. When she sits down, you get a glimpse of her knickers between the buttons. I like the dress. It makes you want to unbutton it (I suppose that's why it's designed that way). One day I drive her home, and she gratefully invites me in to eat bread smeared with tomato. As she's a temp she doesn't have the sense of respect for me a full-timer would. We go to a dark basement bar she knows in her barrio. She orders champagne, but I don't know if it's her usual drink (if she likes it and always asks for it) or if she orders it to indicate it's a special occasion, one to celebrate, as it were, so I know she wants to bed me. Days later I realise she likes champagne a lot and always orders it, but that evening, nonetheless, she ends up back at my house and in my bed. All the time repeating 'slowly does it,' but I suppose it's so I know she knows what she's doing.

Every day, before going to work, I call my wife and speak to the boy. At night I watch television and get dinner ready and don't make any mess. Conversely, I imagine her throwing Spanish omelettes, bottles of wine and crusty bread out of the apartment window.

I get the hots for Dolors like I don't remember feeling for years. I lay her twice in the company disabled toilet. The place where the security guards change and the cleaning ladies keep the toilet rolls and rubbish. There's a kind of bidet with a grille over the top (who knows what the point of that is). While I'm on the floor, belly in the air, I can see the guards' street clothes and shoes.

On the fourteenth day I've been doing it with Dolors, I'm at home drinking Nescafe (we don't have a coffeepot, we don't do coffee) and ruminating, my hopes raised, over the fact she said she wanted to go to a bingo hall 'and spend and spend.' I reckon she wants to play bingo so I see her in different gear: in fishnet tights and high heels. Suddenly, my heart thuds panic-stricken. I spot two rats on the terrace. They are *not* mice. They're chasing each other under the picnic bench, en route to the down-pipe. I suddenly imagine a military school in London – I'm sure it's London – where the soldiers are forced to march touching the wall. They're not allowed to march diagonally across the square. And these rats do exactly that. I run to close the glass door, even though one might have got inside, because I slept with it open wide. I call my wife but her mobile is switched off, she must be on the beach.

I call Enquiries to get the numbers of rat-killing companies and they give me seven. Some have names that are far too appealing, like Rat-Stop. Mostly I get answering machines and others warn they won't be able to come for some time because they've so many beetle infestations to see to. Finally, one promises to come early in the afternoon. I call work but don't tell them the truth. I'm embarrassed, as if I'm to blame for the rats. I say they're coming to de-rat the street and that as chair of the owners' committee I must be there to open the door for them. I think of Dolors and her buttons: don't get horny; she seems just a drag.

In the afternoon, a car with doors covered in images of humanoid rats parks in front of our block. The owner of the haberdashers on the corner comes out and takes a look. I tell the neighbours – mostly elderly – that I saw a rat in the lobby. I don't want them to think the plants on our terrace are the reason for their visits. A youth wearing Wellington boots and gloves and carrying a bucket comes upstairs. First, he inspects the flat. Then goes back to the car and comes back with a sort of butterfly net and a cage. The rats have gone into hiding, but he immediately locates them among the flowerpots. He sees three. (How wretched he finds more than I anticipated.) If he can, he'll catch them, and, if he can't, he'll have to poison them. I pray he catches them. So it's all over and done with. I ask him if there might be any inside. He looks behind the sofa and in the kitchen. He opens the cupboards and sniffs. He says that after all these years he recognises their smell right away. I could never put my head inside a cupboard thinking there might be a rat inside. He doesn't think so, there can't be any, but, just in case, he'll leave a little packet of poison behind the sofa and another in the kitchen. I mustn't touch them. Rats smell the smell of human beings and get very suspicious. Very clever. He tells me lots of things. The drains are bigger in the States, and the rats come up through the lavatories.

'But it only happens in the Bronx, right?' he adds.

When I was a kid I always thought a rat might pop up in the bowl when I was having a crap. (Now *that* is something I wouldn't want the counsellor to know.) The youth goes back on the terrace and I'm a coward and stay inside. He tries intrepidly to catch them, though he doesn't take any chances. He's a young man who wears his hair short with silvery highlights, like Dolors, so I imagine him going out on Saturday night with his friends, and living a normal life, despite his line of work. I get the impression he does this because he can't find anything better to do, though he's become inured to it by now.

He doesn't catch them. From where he's standing he tells me where they climb and disappear to, and starts throwing little bright blue tablets, the size of a bar of chocolate, everywhere. The poison. He grabs the bucket with his gloved hands. He says that once, in an abandoned yard, the rats were so hungry that when he threw the poison around, they jumped on it like dogs. Then he sets a trap. He asks me if I've got any tomatoes. I have. He puts it on the sticky cardboard and places it under the bench. The rat that tries to eat the tomato will get stuck there. If this happens, I have to ring them at once. He re-assures me: he says they're more frightened than I am and that, if I go out on the terrace, they'll hide. It's very unusual for a rat to climb anywhere it can be seen. They only attack in self-defence. When this business is all over I must put a grille over the top of the drainpipe, and make sure I cement it in. He'll come back in a week's time. He says they have a delayed reaction to the poison, but as they are so clever, if one dies, the others won't eat any so this way they'll all eat some. Their blood coagulates and they desiccate, so they won't smell. They die painlessly due to an excess of vitamin K. I find that absurd. I couldn't care less whether they suffer; it's not as if we're talking about dogs.

I don't dare open the windows and, by the end of the day, the house smells stale. I ring my wife but she's not back yet. When I get her that night, she hisses: 'If you've got something important to tell me, why don't you write it down?'

I savour the pleasure of telling her something that can't be put in writing. When I tell her, she gets all worked up and wants to sell the flat immediately.

'No more first-floors, no more, never ever,' she bleats.

The rats reunite us for a second. I tell her I want to kiss her and make love to her. I say 'make love' to please her. She titters faintly: 'So do I,' and adds she'll write me a letter and try to send it from an internet café.

I don't go to the beach-flat at the weekend so as not to leave the house to the rats. When we speak, we tell each other we want 'to make love'. I don't go on the terrace, I just look out, and whenever I spot the bastards (which doesn't take long) I give a start. The plants need watering.

On Monday the young man from the rat-killing firm comes and doesn't find a single corpse. He speaks all the time about 'individuals,' to avoid saying 'rats,' as if it's company policy. When he goes to get the tomato trap, he gives a shout. It's caught a little gecko that's still alive. What a shame. He can't detach it without killing it because its legs and belly have stuck to the card. He puts it in a rubbish bag.

'It's a case for euthanasia,' he says. I'm surprised he says this.

I think of my boy and wife. When you have a boy you always think how terrible it would be if anyone ever hurt him. The youth stares at the down-pipe. The rats have piled up seven or eights bars of poison all around it. (I can see that much from the door). I can't think how they did it with their rat-legs. You can also see rat droppings, like pits from black olives. That means they've eaten.

Back inside, he inspects behind the sofa, where he'd left one of the poison capsules just in case he can see any signs. He can't. He says his job is done, but if I think something's amiss, I can ring them and have the right to another inspection at no extra charge. I ask him to come once more before September, because I won't rest until bodies are found. Just in case, I don't go back to the beach-flat. My wife emails from an internet café she finally found. They're nice and friendly words based on our morning telephone conversations. She jokes. She seems relaxed. 'Did you rescue the orange peel I threw in the rubbish bin?' she asks, for example, alluding to my mania for salvaging.

On the evening of the thirtieth I go to pick them up. Her nose has peeled and the sun has turned her cheeks blotchy. Her hair is an undyed mess.

We load their things in the car and the boy cries because we can't take the inflatable bed. He's grown in a fortnight, which doesn't seem possible. There's a big tailback and he falls asleep straight away, he's so exhausted. The wife and I talk about the rats and selling the flat. We enjoy imagining our new flat. I think everything seems fine again, that we love each other once more. We'll get on much better in a new flat; we'll want it again, maybe.

I stop for petrol. The lorries have already parked for the night. My wife wants a Coke and I offer to go and buy her a can. I really feel like doing it with her. I go into the restaurant and linger for a moment looking at the food. It's late, but people are still eating. Two bikers – their clothes give them away: windcheaters round their necks, leather trousers – are eating Russian salad. This makes me think of Dolors. That day, in the bar, she'd asked for some. I don't have any regrets, as if I associate her with disorder, and the wife and the boy represent order and de-ratting. There are triangular portions of Spanish omelette sliced horizontally, like sandwiches, with a mayonnaise filling. People are putting the dishes to heat in the industrial-looking microwaves, with a metal trim. I buy the Coke, go back to the car and give it to my wife. She opens the can, very cheerful, and asks me not to start up yet. I obey. They're playing a song she knows on the radio – she knows a lot, she's got a good ear – and sings in English. She sips. Offers me some and I take a sip.

'Don't you want any more?'

I don't, so she opens the door and puts the can, that's still pretty full, on the ground. She does it subtly so nobody sees her. I start the car up and drive on to the motorway. For a moment I think I've lost the toll ticket, but she's got it. I remember the almost full can of Coke she abandoned.

'Have you looked at your emails today?' she asks me. I say I tried but couldn't, that sometimes our server doesn't work. She believes me.

We don't say another word until we get home. I stop in front of our block and she gets out with the boy clasped round her neck, asleep – she's much brawnier than me. I go to find a parking space and take a long time, because everybody's back from holidays. We have a parking space but my father uses it in August. I leave the bags in the car and decide to get them in the morning.

My wife gets angry when she sees I've not brought them up, because her creams for removing her face pack are in her toiletries bag and she moans that, if they're stolen, she'll lose a small fortune.

'It stinks like it's been shut up,' she grumbles.

In the end, we don't do anything in bed. It's as if my desire on the motorway had just been an illusion. Perhaps *she* had never desired it at all. That night the boy sleeps with his door shut and we do too, because we're frightened. And in the morning I find a letter on the night table. I read the first sheet.

The next Thursday we go back to our counsellor, who's

also got a tan (I notice she's sunbathed topless). Before we get down to business she asks us things as if we were friends. How's it been, what we've been up to. I don't know why, but I tell her we've had rats. She listens attentively and I surmise my wife feels embarrassed. I go on and on about the rats, about how they're scary, about how you're afraid new ones will come and there will never be an end to them. How you're afraid they'll attack your son. She asks how the list-making routine is going.

'It's much better now,' says my wife.

The counsellor looks at me.

'Much better,' I agree.

The Great Wall

I can't get Joan Dilla, my theatre criticism teacher, out of my head. I like everything about him. The fact he's a writer, his backstreet accent, the bored tone he adopts when lecturing, the drinks he orders in the Uni bar, the out-of-fashion bags under his eyes, or his paunch, now that really drives me crazy.

As soon as I've named and defined my feelings, I start paying him a visit when it's time for tutorials, wearing long dresses and hair-dos increasingly in the style of *The Three Sisters*. The despairing way Dilla corrects my spelling mistakes fills me with desire. If I weren't such a feminine, womanly sort, I'd say I get an erection whenever his red felt tip touches a mistake of mine.

One evening when I finally pluck up courage to give him the stories I've written – his opinion will decide whether I chuck them in the sea or not – Dilla strokes my face. He says he's just booked a taxi and can easily drop me off in Barcelona. We can talk about them en route.

But he doesn't open his mouth on the drive and when we say goodbye he only says: 'See you tomorrow, Tam?'

The fact he called me 'Tam' rather than 'Tamara' seems so romantic my eyes water. I open the front door and can see from the reflection in the glass that the taxi's still waiting. Dilla's so concerned about me that he's afraid I might be raped and has told the taxi-driver to wait. I go upstairs and put my neck under the tap to try to cool my hot flushes. There's no way out: I worship him. I now see I wasn't really in love with the other two writers I picked up during my

23

degree. (That was only sex.)

The following day I go to class dressed like Irina, the young sister, in the scene where she feels like sailing a boat under a blue sky. But Dilla behaves as if he hadn't taken me home and said: 'See you tomorrow, Tam?' On the contrary: I'd say he acts rather coldly.

But after a week of keeping his distance, he suggests we go to a bar and talk about my stories, now he's had time to read them. We make an appointment for Saturday night, which I interpret as a good sign: if he didn't want to take me to bed or hadn't liked the stories, we wouldn't be meeting outside class. So at the weekend, rather than going to the country with my three flatmates, I stay in Barcelona. What's more, since I fell in love with Dilla (and now I've got a date with him I feel on fire), I've been faithful to him. I don't intend ever again crossing the threshold of those bars in the old Gothic quarter, haunts of Erasmus students reputed to be easy lays. By ten o'clock on Friday night, I'm already in bed. I'm devouring Dilla's book: *From Barcino to Barcelona, getting to know the Roman city (with itineraries under three hours)*. I hug my pillow (that symbolises Dilla) and kiss it passionately. I take his specs off and put a tit in his mouth. Then the other. He worries about his paunch, not realising it's what I want to hug. I go down on him and frolic. I alternate sweet kisses with the dirtiest sucks. I go turtle-mouthed: I shield my teeth with my lips, so I don't hurt him, and suck. Then nibble gently. Hold it like a microphone and rub it very quickly up and down my lips that go numb. I lick round it in circles and take it whole in my mouth, as far as my uvula. Tears stream down but Dilla likes it a lot when I say: 'Look: you've made me cry.' I run my hand up and down, an andante that soon turns into a prestíssimo the like you've never seen before. Without letting go of his knob (never ever, it's a rule I imposed on myself right from the start), I bring my head out from under the sheet and take a breath of air (it's very hot down there; men never take that into account). 'Dilla, are you bothered that I'm still left-handed?' I ask him naïvely. For some reason, this precipitates events. But I don't swallow the outcome, I keep it in my mouth. So, when Dilla comes to, I can tell him to take a look, I spit it along his body and swallow it whole again.

He then apologises for coming so quickly, because it seems he felt more excited than ever. As I don't want him to feel frustrated, I arouse him again. I go face down and suggest – to my Dilla-pillow – that he enters from the rear. He can't believe his ears, but I don't need to repeat myself. He starts to saliva me up and clings to my hair. While I shriek (pain and pleasure, one imagines), I think for a moment how if our relationship becomes public knowledge in the Faculty, he won't go to jail. At the most, he'll get a reprimand.

After all we've gone through I feel lethargic, and put my bra back on (I sleep in my bra because I want these pretty breasts of mine to keep firm into old age). But before going to sleep, I plan everything I've got to buy, given that, if we do anything, you can be sure it will be here, in my place, because he lives with his wife and daughter. He's mentioned his wife four times: three neutrally, and once praising her, if condescendingly. He always speaks well of his daughter. (I'm sure that if everything goes as it should, we'll be close friends. She's my age.)

In the morning I go to the Chinese shop and buy two ice-trays and a set of six long glasses. I buy a bottle of the Irish whisky Dilla likes from the off-licence. When I get back to the flat, I pour a drop down the toilet so he doesn't notice I've only just opened the bottle: I fill the ice-trays, frantically clean the bedroom, change the sheets and for the first time use a pillow-case my mother gave me for Christmas, spread the condoms around they gave out on campus for World Aids Day (so they seem less premeditated than if they came from the chemists), I depilate and wash myself with vaginal soap. (Although it destroys the flora. So what? As if it's exterminating it.)

We said we'd meet in front of the police station on Via Laietana. My choice may appear random, but not really. Most of the lecturers in the faculty talk about being tortured in this police station during the Franco dictatorship. Whether it's true or not, telling their story makes them go all soft. Besides, there are Roman ruins in the neighbourhood and I know – from the little experience I've had with this kind of intellectual – that in no city in the world will you bed a man as quickly as in Barcelona, if you show an interest in its Roman ruins. On this occasion I'm wearing a white lacy dress I bought in the second-hand market, just right for the scene in the garden.

I park my bike and he greets me with a wave of my manuscript. (I get butterflies.) He gives me two kisses and asks: 'How are you?'

I go as red as a tomato. I'm embarrassed to talk to him, for no reason whatever, after doing all I did to him (in pillow form) the night before.

'All right.'

'Shall we go for a drink? To The Future or The Galician?'

My god. What do I say now? I nod, as if just answering the first part of his question. He's named two places that say a lot about the kind of man he is. The Future is a modern bar with a grey tiled floor where people drink glasses but not bottles of wine. The Galician is a bar with a set menu that has only recently become trendy among artists because you can play cards or chess. What shall I say? The Future or the Galician? Perhaps I should act humble and say the Galician. But if we go to the Galician my clothes and hair will stink of fry-ups. On the other hand, if I say The Future, I'll seem more modern than I really am and risk Dilla making fun of my background as a rich girl whose daddy pays her way through university. Besides, hopefully he'll be inviting me, but what if he doesn't? Will I have enough cash if we go to The Future?

'You choose, you choose!' He can choose for the whole

of eternity.

'OK, let's go to the Galician.'

Shit. Now I'll have to take a shower when we get home. And we've got an electric heater; the water takes half an hour to get lukewarm. I'll have to change my knickers and bra, but I've only got one cotton set; the one I'm wearing. When I went to the Erasmus bars I'd wear silk and synthetic so as not to look too young. Going to the Galician has messed everything up. I should have dared to go for The Future.

'Petty crime is on the increase,' he tells me.

'The Town Hall just couldn't care less about anything,' I respond, neatly demonstrating my mental agility. I get the impression he supports the party in power, but is on the critical wing. If he says petty crime is increasing, it must be because he doesn't agree with the mayor's immigration policy, right?'

'Do you vote?' he asks, taking me by surprise.

I think the question about The Future or The Galician was relatively more straightforward. What do I say? If he doesn't vote and I say I do, I look like a student who follows the herd and has sold out to the system. He'll reproach me for not being a rebel, and obeying rules. On the other hand, if I say I don't and he's one of these fanatical democrats who always vote, I'll look bad even if I give him the best anarchist arguments as to why I don't. He'll criticise me for sitting on the fence and wanting everything on a plate. Something like that might defer my chances of bedding him *sine die*, as he says in class. Obviously I could say I vote, and then if it turns out he doesn't, add that I put in a blank slip. I risk it: 'Yes, I'm going to.'

'I don't. I know I should, but...' He says this rather guiltily, so I adapt my strategy.

'Well, I suppose I think if I don't vote, I'll have no right to complain about the system later on.'

I look him in the face. Bingo. Half past seven. Still on cue. Bed's on again. I'll take his clothes off, I'll kiss him all over, I'll put my ear to his hairy paunch and listen to his gastric juices and I'll get and will give orgasms that will make him whimper nostalgically every night when he sleeps with his wife. When I'm stark naked, he'll see I'm a nymph like the ones we study in class, a fairy, Wendla deep down in the woods. And perhaps he'll even say I've got the talent to become a writer and he'll help me publish my stories. He'll take me to the most expensive eateries in New York. We'll drink in hotel bars and rented rooms. He'll introduce me to his writer friends so they die of envy.

'You're right.'

I smile modestly and, to avoid having to tell him whom I vote for, I create a diversion and complain about the refuse: 'Look at all the rubbish. The fact is…'

'This must be the most neglected historical quarter in the whole of Europe.'

He's done it again! His every word is a time bomb about to explode. Am I up to speed with Europe's neglected historic quarters? Not Paris; does London have one? Madrid even less so. Cáceres doesn't count, because it's a Heritage site.

'Too true,' I reply in the end. I casually pat him on the arm. 'The one in Naples is much cleaner.'

He clicks his fingers several times acknowledging I'm right too and asks: 'Feel like a bite?' This time I know what to answer from his tone of voice.

'No,' I lie. 'I'd not given it a thought.' But I do. Who isn't hungry at 10pm? Perhaps Dilla is used to writing at night, never has supper and just drinks whisky.

We stroll on. He has a slight limp because he twisted his ankle playing football. He's the kind of man who plays football with his friends in his barrio: friends who are postmen or mechanics. He points things out as we walk: a square that was bombed during the Civil War or a balcony that still preserves distinctive medieval guild tiles intact. My eyes feel like they do when I drink sparkling water. I love him. I want to spend my whole life being his muse and never

ever have dinner.

'If you like, I'll show you the Roman wall,' he suggests. I whoop enthusiastically that I do, oh, I do. We head for Via Laietana. We see some imposing façades and patrician gravestones. I could murder him with my kisses here and now. I feel at melting point. This time I won't abort if I get pregnant.

'Look at that!' And he points at a side road that ends in a kind of wall that's covered in graffiti.

I try not to commit myself. Look interested but neutrally so. For the moment I haven't a clue what he wants to show me.

'This is a fragment of the wall,' he explains. And suddenly acts as if he's really happy. He suddenly yelps because he's seen a friend. A friend who's also enjoying the wall – something that could happen nowhere else in the world. They insult each other, shout, joke, and in a more backstreet tone than ever: 'Prick-artist!'

'Lick–my–arse.'

'You bugger!'

'But what the fuck you doing here?'

The last sentence, as he pronounces it, sounds like: 'B't wat t'fuck yer doin' here?'

Lick–my–arse is walking arm in arm with a girl I know by sight because she used to study in my faculty (I remember vaguely that her name's Penelope Picó and she's stupid). I don't think, on the other hand, that he ever taught me. I'd remember him, because he's not bad at all, and he also limps as if it were a generational trait. Penelope is all over me. She's wearing red striped tights, dark brown, light brown, and green, metal buckled shoes and a black felt hat. She's dressed in what she must reckon is a little witch's outfit. Bet they tell her she's like a little witch. We kiss each other and say 'what a coincidence' as the two men separate out to talk. You can see one asking the other who I am, and if he's laid me. (That really turns me on.) I gradually recall stuff about our

Penelope: that she dropped out in the third year because she was anorexic and never came to class.

'This is really crazy,' she exclaims as she plaits some strands of her hair. 'We'd given up introducing women to Joan.'

Immediately, though we hardly know each other, she takes my arm (she's one of these women who think physical contact is *terrifically* important) and runs through her sad fling with Lick-my-arse. The girl had an internship in the sports supplement of the daily he works for. First she just admired him, but admiration soon turned into something much more profound. Nobody had any sympathy for her – the paper is so macho and conservative – and her relationship with that married writer (he's a writer) whose meniscus had been operated on (hence the limp).

'I need to learn from a man,' she emphasises passionately. 'I want to suck them dry, be a sponge, want them to give me their all.'

And she repeats that she wants to suck them dry. And also repeats she is a *baby*, that she knows she's only a baby, but people of her own age don't *do* anything for her, because they are so immature, so infantile, etc. Those her age live so *removed* from literary circles…

I can see that all she wants in life is to stumble on a chick in the same boat (who's a goer like herself) who can give her support, advice and lend her clothes. She's already loving me and taking me on. She immediately interrupts the two men to tell them in a tone as upbeat as it is hollow: 'Joan, I really like this little woman. You know I'm a bit of a witch and never get it wrong.'

Lick nods and smiles weakly: 'You're very nice, you know.' But he doesn't say what his name is. Nobody thinks of introducing us.

When Dilla announces that we were going to eat in the Galician, they immediately join the party. And when he says we were walking around the wall to get up an appetite, Lick's panda-ish eyes light up. He is in fact – Dilla knows only too well – the author of a book on daily life between the 1st and 4th centuries AD, and if he adores anything, it's the wall. As we all now limp along, he adds grinning heroically: 'The fact is we are homeless today. Thanks for adopting us…'

Penelope takes me by the arm again and eagerly tells me more. She imagines his wife knows he has a lover (Penelope), because Lick is very sincere and hides nothing (he'd be incapable). His marriage has been a farce for a long time. But his wife – Penelope dubs her 'the Valkyrie' – not only makes his life impossible, but, following the advice of her female lawyer, she's hoping he'll 'abandon the hearth' so she gets everything. As a result, the poor guy can't leave the house or go to buy a box of matches, except on a Saturday, when he says he's on the night shift and spends Saturday night with her in a hotel. It's the only day they see each other. Bored, I listen to her chatter, while Dilla and his friend walk on in front, as happy as ever. They stop on each corner and, from time to time, turn round: 'We're infatuated with these stones. Please do forgive us…' says one.

'Please don't abandon us… We know we're very trying,' says the other.

I smile, but frankly I'm starting to get the wind up. It's one thing to go for a stroll with Dilla (as a step prior to going to bed and a step prior to him telling me my stories are masterpieces) and quite another to go for a stroll with Dilla and that couple.

'It's amazing,' fawns Lick. 'They've become super friends.'

'It's scary. Now they'll start criticising us,' the other replies equally cheerily. 'They'll be saying: "Those two old guys have got a couple of choice chicks waiting on them and they're not giving them the time of day." What you bet me?'

'Hey, hey, hey, wait a minute! What do you think we're going to do?' asks Penelope as she twists another plait. (Fiddling with her hair up is a fad of hers).

Everybody laughs, except for me. They're quite capable of wanting to spend the night drinking mulled cognac and reciting poems. We stop in a square that's only very recently been done up and wonder at the half walls of demolished apartment buildings that have been left.

'I love to see a building showing its entrails… the different tiles in the toilets and wallpaper in the living-rooms,' Dilla trills passionately.

'It's like seeing a slice of daily life we're being shown quite shamelessly…' continues Lick. 'The small tiles, the beams, the imprint of the stairs…'

'The traces of a picture frame on a wall…'

'A calendar…'

'A tap…'

When they've stopped slavering, Lick comes over to Penelope – who displays her best 'I'm so sensitive and moved' girly face – and embraces her. He kisses her noisily, and out of empathy Dilla follows suit. I press myself against him and for a moment lose sight of the world. When we disentangle, Lick and Chick look at each other like a couple of toads.

Both men start to show off how aroused they are. They hide nothing. They want the world to know.

'To our old age…!' one chants.

'We are very lucky,' the other acknowledges. As if I am already Dilla's official girlfriend and it's only a matter of moments before we agree on a time and day for the foursome to make its escape to Paris.

We continue strolling but now as couples. We walk down a side road and look at the Roman ruins that are under the civic centre.

'Watch out!' Penelope warns her Lick, from time to time.

'What?' he asks, all sensitive.

'You were about to tread on some dog-poo.'

'I'd seen it…!' he laments, as if not seeing a dog turd made him someone less knowledgeable and less sensitive in

32

respect of the realities of this Barcelona he loves so much. Sometimes, they half row over things like this.

I feel my feet are badly swollen. (The three sisters wear boots with heels, but they don't move from the Prokhorovs throughout the play, and the longest journey they go on is behind the screen to change their clothes.) I calculate there must be a good kilometre or two left, and my desire to bed Dilla is waning slightly. I just want to eat a hamburger with lashings of mustard and take my shoes off. On the other hand, limps and all, the two men are as fresh as daisies. They behave as if they could never stop discussing the Roman ruins. I now see it all: Hollywood played a bad trick on them, a really cruel hand, when it produced a film for the masses on the sinking of the Titanic. The sinking of the Titanic, when it was strictly for buffs must have stirred them even more.

'It's incredible. It's gob-smacking…' Dilla exclaims pointing out a balcony. And in a flash he's turning to me apologetically: 'I'm sorry. You must think I'm mad, and so very rude.'

'We are. We are. We are so very rude,' adds the other. 'Penelope and I haven't seen each other for five days and this is *our* night.'

It was predictable. They have *their* night. And I'd bet a nipple on them also having their bar, their song, their day, their lucky number, their colour, their poem, their city and their hotel. They're the kind who must celebrate the anniversary of their first fuck, fuck number two, number twenty and the day they finished their first box of condoms. And in a week's time they'll also want to celebrate the fact they've known *us* for a week.

A Pakistani offers us roses, and the idiot Penelope, rather than saying no and not looking at him, goes and smiles at him. After she's given him a way in, the enchantress can't get him off our backs. He hovers behind us until Lick softens and decides to buy a rose for Penelope and one for me, as I am so special. Dilla insists on paying and takes his wallet out, but has to search around to find a few cents. He finally asks me for a spare euro. Watch it, fella.

By the time we get to the Galician, the kitchen's been shut half an hour.

'The Future will be the same,' predicts Penelope. And she tells us she didn't have lunch. She's not anorexic anymore, but I surmise that, as a consequence, she's now one who likes to miss out meals and then go hungry at odd times of day. And when this happens, they always want a *tapa* and a glass of champagne, but always go into the wrong bars that don't sell champagne by the glass. The four of us stand rooted to the spot pondering our next move. We can't go to Lick's, or to Dilla's, because their wives are at home. Penelope's place is not on: she lives with her parents (and they have always been *awfully* liberal, but they wouldn't understand), so Dilla suggests going to my place. Lick thinks that a very exciting idea and tries to persuade me: 'Look, Pe and I will take a taxi and get some food from the petrol station.'

'But I'm not sure I'm up to riding on one of those infernal engines known as motorbikes,' Dilla warns him, pompously.

'Hey! Get that headline: "Joan Dilla Rides Motorbike for the First Time",' jokes Penelope.

I am not at all amused. I can't stand the idea of carrying a man as a pillion-rider (who's going to go to bed with me). If I'd liked carrying men, I wouldn't have stopped going to Erasmus bars. I wouldn't be an (unpublished!) writer. I wouldn't dress like Irina, I'd buy my clothes from System Action. Besides, this means we can't talk about my stories.

'Joan, you'll have to dare! You can't abandon this young lady!' the other chides him.

Nor am I very keen on preparing sandwiches for four, or opening up Vanessa's bedroom so Lick and Chick can spend their night there. I don't want a communal shower and breakfast in the morning just before Lick rushes home pretending he's finished his shift. But I've no choice; the three of them are already limping towards Via Laietana. I walk behind and listen to them making their plans. The Licks will now go to Seven Eleven and buy wine, whisky, champagne, baguettes, sausage and everything to *improvise* supper, and the improvised supper has clearly dirty resonances for them. And if they were so lucky that there weren't enough chairs at my place and they had to sit on the floor or on the bed, I could see them having a wonderful time. This is much more fun for them than sex. I envisage Lick and Chick on their way to Seven Eleven ready to buy the improvised supper, and see they are verging on ecstasy. She finally gets out a pencil and pad to jot down everyone's orders:

'*S'il vous plaît*, who wants tonic water and what brand?' she squeaks. But he's already stopped a taxi.

'Take down my address,' I tell her.

'Don't get lost on the way!' adds Dilla cheekily.

Once we're alone, we limp parsimoniously up Via Laietana to the police-station, where I'd parked my bike. Now if Dilla were a man he'd take me to a hotel. Here and now. He'd grab me, take me violently by the neck and say not to worry about his friends, they'll understand. He'd also say my stories are masterpieces and must be published immediately, something that would be good for both of us. But he just pinches me on the cheek and exclaims grimacing: 'Yeah… let me fuck you!' while we walk at a donkey-pace.

By the time it takes us to cross to my bike, I calculate the Licks must have bought everything. I search for my keys in my bag while looking wistfully at all the bars and restaurants that are open. I detach the spare helmet and give it to him to put on, but it doesn't fit. I now see he's got a big head.

'Great, at last I can put my arms round you…' he whispers after squeezing it on with great difficulty. He says this as if it were the Most Perverted Saying of the Year.

I start up, kick the stand up and bend the bike towards the kerb so I can get on. Poor man, his joints are all creaky and there's no way he can get his leg over. Seeing this any scrap of desire I had left to strip his clothes off disappears.

I put my foot down, and he clings to me, because he's scared. He's like a little girl. I head up Via Laietana and stop at the traffic lights. Taken by surprise, his helmet hits mine. He's not used to riding pillion and throws himself on me, out of lack of habit. He takes up more than half my seat. Whenever I accelerate, quite unawares he bangs into me. With each bang, I get more annoyed. I count them: one, two, three, four… If he does it again, my hatred will be savage, merciless, out-of-this-world. He hits into me again. I'd leave him there if it weren't for my stories and because he'd fail me. I brake on purpose, and he crashes into me again. I can't help thinking that Lick and Chick must be in my doorway by now, sitting on the doorstep, surrounded by brimful plastic bags, laughing, safe and sound, hugging to keep the cold off, eating crisps and drinking Coke, filling in the time, waiting for the entertainment to arrive.

The Interpretation of Dreams

'I dreamed about you today.'

'Oh really?'

'I dreamed I caught you in bed with another man.'

Plàcid the librarian weighs the situation up. The sentence his boyfriend has just uttered will lead ineluctably to a row. There's no way round that. Whatever he says, in ten minutes they'll be rowing. He'd better prepare himself.

Plàcid the librarian got to know his boyfriend through a personal ad. It was a day he'd not been drinking but, even so, he thought he was the handsomest man on earth. They hooked up. However, the relationship's into its seventh month and, in all this time, Plàcid the librarian has rowed more than ever before. They row all the time, at the slightest excuse. Smashing plates or not. In civilised fashion or like savages. Waking up the neighbours or not. His boyfriend prefers rows to sex, food, surfing on the Internet and, even, showing photographs of himself from before he went bald.

Today they dined out to celebrate the fact they were back on speaking terms after the last row. So Plàcid the librarian trod lightly. He didn't contradict him, didn't smile at the waiter and didn't bat an eyelid, when his boyfriend made categorical, self-important statements. To conceal his boredom, he said he felt off-colour, and wasn't all over the black public relations guy in the bar where they are now, with whom he'd had an occasional fling some time back. But he now sees it was to no avail because his boyfriend has been brewing a row from early on. He'd predicted this. Plàcid the librarian decides it's a lost cause. He can perfectly well anticipate what will happen next.

If he replies: 'You can't be fed up with me because of the dream…' The other will say: 'Did I say I was fed up with you because of that dream?' Placid the librarian will retort: 'But you're looking daggers at me…' And his boyfriend's response will be 'I'm looking daggers because I'm annoyed you say I'm fed up with you because of that dream.' Etcetera.

If Plàcid the librarian says: 'But it's not my fault,' his boyfriend will go silent on him. He'll tug the four hairs of his goatee – fair going on red – and shake his head knowingly; an attitude he likes to strike of being both offended and incredulous. Plàcid the librarian will ask: 'What's wrong?' And he will stiffen and act all surprised: 'Wrong with me? What on earth's going to be wrong with me?' Plàcid the librarian will come back: 'You're not talking to me, I think you're angry with me.' The other will look him up and down: '*Ought* I perhaps to be angry?' Plàcid the librarian will ask why and his boyfriend will act all surprised again: 'I don't know. You were the one who said I was. Not me.' Etcetera.

Of course, he could look as if he's sorry. But he's not. It's hardly his fault if his boyfriend dreams he's being unfaithful. Besides, if he acts as if he's sorry, the other will only take it further. He'll connect the hassle over the dream to some hassle from way back. He's very clever at running one row in to another, and another. He'll move on from the dream to the time Plàcid the librarian stared at a man in the street. And from there to the day he admired the eyes of the Channel Three newsreader. Etcetera.

He could retort, lucky it was only a dream. But he'll get really upset. Will say: 'You taking the piss? You treating me like an idiot because I was honest with you? I know it's not your fault that I dream what I dream, but it's not mine either. Or do you think I'm doing it for fun? Maybe if I dream like that, it's because you're pushing me that way. Because you've turned me into someone who feels insecure.' Etcetera.

What will happen if he ironically begs for forgiveness? What will happen if he grovels: 'I'm a poor wretch! Please forgive me! I had a bit on the side in a dream!' Perhaps this will make him laugh and avoid a row. No chance. He only laughs at his own jokes. It could only delay things. If Plàcid the librarian grovels: 'I'm a poor wretch! Please forgive me! I had a bit on the side in a dream!' He'll grin and retort: 'Only in a dream? Have you never had an extra-marital affair?' If he defends himself with a 'no way,' his boyfriend will mutter: 'It's so revealing the way you suddenly turn serious when only half a minute ago you were all jokey.' Etcetera.

If, on the other hand, instead of defending himself with a 'no way,' he says: 'I'm having a bit on the side all the time'; his boyfriend will answer: 'That's great. Can you name names?' He'll say yes, continuing in the same tone. Yes, he can name names, because he's bedding all the neighbours, including the owner of the gay salted fish shop next door to Plàcid the librarian's block, the one who is so ugly. His boyfriend will react, slowly: 'And I suppose David's also one of the ones you're loosening up. Don't forget him.' Now they'll slip into the argument about how he's lusting after David the discotheque bouncer. David the bouncer is in fact the person who triggered off their last squabble.

On the other hand, if Plàcid the librarian responds in hurt tones: 'Come on! Don't tell me you're feeling shirty because of a dream!' things will deteriorate quickly. His boyfriend will snarl: 'Sorry if I offended you, OK?' He'll retort: 'I don't feel offended…' And he will counter-attack: 'Nobody'd believe you. You got so very defensive.' 'So very defensive?' 'Yes, so very defensive.' 'I didn't get so very defensive, I only said you can't start feeling shirty because of a dream.' 'So why do I detect something strange in your tone of voice?' Etcetera. Etcetera.

There's no way out. He was about to go home, would have finished his drink in twenty minutes, changed his clothes and gone out to dance to Eighties music at the Marlene with his friend, Carmen the librarian. Now he'll have to squabble till 4am. Because whichever of the potential rows he goes for, will lead to reprimands, silences, long faces, tears and frowns. In the end his boyfriend will walk out of the bar in a huff – it's a favourite trick of his to get out of paying. There's only one way to avoid a row: for the waiter to have a heart attack. By the time they help him, look for his little box of pills, give him artificial respiration, phone the Gay Guide, ask for an ambulance and the police take a statement from them, it will be 4am. And his boyfriend gets sleepy at 4am. None of their rows ever starts at 5am. He's done for by four. He can also avoid it if a homophobe now comes in the bar, calls them all perverts, makes them stretch out on the floor and – attracted by the guild's pink purchasing power – robs, insults and beats them. And he can also avoid it if he can get his boyfriend to start explaining, yet again, how he wants to be a writer, and that he's got a novel in his head about his first sexual experience, because the things that have happened *to him* are right out of the pages of a novel. He only has to put it on paper, but doesn't because the world of publishing is a stitch-up and it's very difficult for a person with no influence to get published. And because he's not like the rest, he's got high standards. In fact, he thinks he can write much better than the *pretentious* stuff that does get into print.

But Plàcid the librarian can't now ask him, all casual-like: 'Hey, how's that novel on your first sexual experience going?' If he does, he'll say: 'You're brilliant at changing the subject. Maybe you're changing the subject because you feel guilty…' Etcetera.

He opens his mouth to respond. He'd sell his soul for one of his boyfriend's exes to enter the bar. Then Plàcid the librarian could show he's jealous and maybe by going on the attack could stall *his* attack. But it's a very remote possibility. If an ex of his boyfriend walks in and sees him, he'll turn tail and head to another bar to avoid a row with him. What can he say? He's sorry? It's not his fault? It *is* his fault? How can he get wound up over something like this? The second option is the quickest route. The row will start earlier. But that doesn't mean it will necessarily finish earlier. Oh no. If the row gets off to an early start, his boyfriend never lets up. He's used to arguing with his mother and you bet his mother always ends up giving way. His boyfriend sees himself as a 'cynic'. He's proud of it too. But his kind of cynicism is straight out of the American soaps with heterosexual couples he so likes. It's about making grand-sounding statements larded with comparisons and jokes about facial tics, in a slightly falsetto voice, and eyes askew.

'You know what? No need to answer that,' his boyfriend laughs. But he laughs like that when he's already taken offence. 'Anyone else, anyone normal, would have asked for detail. Who you were deceiving me with in the dream, and whether I was having a really bad time, if we sorted it out or not. Would have said: 'I'd never do a thing like that to you.' But you don't, because I know *you* would. And have already in the past. And if you'd deceive me in real life, it would be even worse in a dream. It's funny because you reacted as only *you* could react. When I caught you, you told me I'd get a good financial settlement. You love reproducing hetero roles in my dreams. It's not just that you've decorated your house like a hetero; you're much more hetero than you think.'

This is the worst possible outcome.

'I don't reproduce hetero roles,' he protests. 'I've not decorated my house like a hetero.'

'Aren't kitchen curtains patterned with fruit sliced down the middle hetero? Isn't offering me a financial settlement after being unfaithful adopting a hetero role?'

'But I didn't.'

'We're talking about what reproducing a hetero role is all about. Not whether you were or weren't. Did I say you were? Perhaps in the event you wouldn't. Perhaps you'd just ditch me in the street.'

41

'I couldn't ditch you like that. You live with your parents.'

'So don't say you don't reproduce hetero roles. I don't think it's a problem, by the way. You treat me like a high-class tart.'

'But you can't blame me because of a dream.'

'Am I blaming you? I'm amazed. You're putting words into my mouth.'

'Let's drop the subject.'

'Ah, let's drop the subject. You couldn't care less if I wake up in tears, if I feel miserable, if I've been feeling low all today. The gentleman wants to drop the subject because he couldn't care less.'

'No, I do care.'

'Sorry, I just don't get you. You do care, but you want us to drop the subject. Is that it?'

Plàcid the librarian knows his boyfriend can bleat on in this fashion non-stop for an hour. He gets up: 'I'm going for a piss.'

'Fantastic.'

'What do you mean "fantastic"?'

'Going for a piss is always the way you sort things.'

Plàcid the librarian sits down again. There's no escape. Just be patient, ask the waiter for another gin and tonic, knock it back and order another. He raises his arm to call him over, but then sees the bottle of Bombay gin, the brand he wanted, fall to the ground. The others crash into each other. The empty glasses on the bar, the stools, the 60s lights decorating the bar start to shake. First, he ignores what's happening. He imagines the metro must run underneath. But the tables fall over, the lights go out and everyone starts shouting. The floor cracks and the ceiling collapses.

When he comes to he feels his face is wet and, in a state of shock, he assumes it must be blood. There are lumps of concrete all around. It must have been an earthquake. Or an explosion. He gradually starts remembering. They were rowing and got buried under rubble. He hears his boyfriend calling to him, asking if he's all right and dragging himself over to where he is. He blacks out, but is woken by slaps on his cheeks. He recognises the way his boyfriend slaps. He hears coughing and crying. A man is moaning 'Ay, ay, ay,' as if it were a litany. His boyfriend calls for help and hugs him, as best he can.

Plàcid the librarian smiles. He's been spared the row. When they rescue them they'll be taken to hospital, then from hospital home. There'll be psychologists specialising in disaster therapy who will recommend rest. He's thinking about this while he listens to dogs bark, sirens, the thuds of those searching for signs of life. He's been spared the row. He can't believe his luck.

'Here!' shouts his boyfriend. He groans in pain.

And suddenly, a man who identifies himself as a fireman, assures them through a megaphone that they'll get them out. He hears his boyfriend answering questions. He's saying that Plàcid the librarian's leg is trapped (he hadn't noticed) and his face is covered in blood. He also hears the fireman advising his boyfriend not to let Plàcid the librarian fall asleep. Talk to him. Amuse him. But don't let him fall asleep.

His boyfriend takes his hand. He tidies his hair away from his forehead: 'Keep it up. They'll soon get us out,' he promises. You heard him say you mustn't fall asleep. I know you're very tired but you've got to keep awake. They'll get us out within the hour. Don't move, you can't move, the fireman said so. He said I must talk to you. And that's strange because I really feel like talking to you. I can't stop thinking about my dream. I feel betrayed, I feel dirty. I hate remembering you gyrating in bed with that guy. Don't fall sleep, whatever you do.'

Women's Day

Downcast, the six women who make up the executive committee of the Euterpe Association look at the individual walking through the entrance to the cultural centre, who has most definitely come to collect one of the Women's Prizes. The individual is not a woman.

'Enriqueta Borrull?' asks the individual. 'I'm Miquel from Act against Hunger.'

He's wearing jeans and a T-shirt emblazoned with one black sheep in a flock of white. He also sports blue-framed spectacles, long sideburns, a pencil moustache and a tuft under his lip.

'What on earth has happened?' shouts a redheaded Euterpe. 'Where's the woman who was going to come?'

'What woman?' he asks. He puts the slide-screen he was carrying on his shoulder on the floor and slips off the rucksack containing a projector. He wipes away the sweat from his bald pate with a tissue and runs his teeth over his tuft. He attempts to justify his presence: a representative of the Euterpe Women phoned his NGO and informed them they'd been awarded the Silver Woman for the aid work they do in Guinea. But didn't inform them the person who collected the prize had to be a woman. Scandalised, the red-haired Euterpe shakes her head: 'Come on, you take that for granted!'

Another Euterpe comes over. She's wearing a security guard's uniform as if she's come straight from work. She's in her mid-forties, stout, and her hair is cut very short and colourless though the roots are dark.

'It should be obvious women must predominate in an act celebrating Women's Day, and that a prize against sexism is for women.' She adjusts her belt-buckle. 'If you men take this over as well…'

He repeats his excuses. If they'd been told, it wouldn't have been a problem, quite the contrary, to send a woman instead of him, because he's not an administrator, just an aid-worker; he makes it very plain he's not come to be in the spotlight, he's come on behalf of Guinea, and is not interested in prizes or kudos. But he shuts up and runs his teeth back over his tuft, because the Euterpe women now start to shout in horror. The next individual to walk into the cultural centre is wearing a Palestinian scarf round his neck, baggy trousers slung low Arab-fashion and backless peasant-style sandals. His hair is long and fair. He's no woman either.

'Marc Fluvià,' he introduces himself. 'I'm here on behalf of Labour for Women.'

'I am Enriqueta Borrull…' mumbles a slightly-built Euterpe, with round spectacles and short grey hair. But she moves her cheek away when he goes to kiss her. She offers him a hand instead.

'It's incredible the sexism still around in the world…' complains the security guard, as if speaking to herself. 'You are still blotting us out.'

'We ought to be women,' explains the tufted aid-worker.

The third person to cross the threshold is carrying her slide projector and screen in a shopping trolley. She's slim and highly freckled and doesn't depilate the fluff above her upper lip. A woman. At last.

'I am Magda Carmona, from Women Journalists for Equality,' she greets them.

The Euterpes shower her in grateful kisses.

'If I'd known there was going to be a projector, I wouldn't have brought mine,' she complains.

'If you want, we can share,' says the tufted aid-worker

straight away.

Meanwhile, the other guy is scrutinising the murals that decorate the hall, with such concentration he might be correcting spelling mistakes. From time to time, he nods approvingly.

'Well, why not,' responds the female aid-worker. 'It's rather absurd to set up two projectors.'

She says this dryly and the aid-worker with the tuft replies in the same tone: 'Quite right, that's why I said what I said. It would be absurd.'

'Where are your pics from?'

'From Guinea, and yours?'

'Afghanistan.'

Forty minutes after the official starting-time – with an audience of nineteen women in the hall – the Mayoress arrives. Very flustered she greets the prizewinners and sits at the table next to an Euterpe. She welcomes the audience on behalf of the city council. She slips a green plastic ring off her thumb and puts it on top of her file, separates out the volumised wisps of her fringe, as if applying hair cream, lifts the microphone to her mouth, asks if people can hear her and says she will comment briefly on the philosophy behind the prizes.

She rehearses a little of the history, reminds everyone that the mothers and grandmothers in the Euterpe women's group, all inhabitants of that city, were feminists *avant la lettre* – she pauses, after saying this – and adds that she's particularly happy she can now call on Manoli to contribute, the Euterpe on her left, who's only recently been re-incorporated into society. Euterpe Manoli wipes her bleary eyes on her T-shirt, a black sleeveless T-shirt, with the imprint of a grey lamp. She gulps a mouthful of beer from a can, puts it on the Mayoress's pile of papers and starts reading a text in the first person, as if the person speaking was the muse Euterpe. But air leaks from a carious incisor and the Mayoress instinctively backs away from her. Enriqueta Borrull, sitting in the audience, keeps nodding her head to encourage her whenever she stumbles.

'I am proud to read this statement,' she recites finally. 'I have begun no wars. I don't issue sentences of death. I don't practice gender violence. I am a housewife, I am a professional, I am lesbian, I am retired, I am an ex-junkie, I am HIV positive, I am Afghan, I am Guinean. I am a …woman!'

Three spectators struggle to keep their eyes open, and two women get up surreptitiously and leave. The others talk among themselves.

'Silence, please…' demands the Mayoress. And immediately introduces the fair-haired speaker who will collect the Golden Woman Prize.

'Yes, hi,' he responds. And ties his hair with a rubber band. The muttering stops at once.

'Hey, handsome!' shouts an adolescent punk, sitting on a desk.

The Mayoress goes all giggly and titters.

He looks down modestly and makes it clear he is not an aid-worker but an administrator. For NGOs also need people around to handle their resources. And this is important work, though less showy than working in the field. (When they hear this, the other two speakers shake their heads in horror.) Consequently, he has brought facts rather than slides. Boring facts. But necessary facts.

The audience look at him enraptured. And for the twenty minutes he takes to tell them the number of women who appear on the front-pages of daily newspapers and the number of men who loom large in soap powder adverts, they eye up his mountaineer's bracelets, his necklace and a silvery half moon pendant and his long, smooth hair. They stare at his thick chapped lips, his dark shrimp-coloured gums, and small, seemingly milk teeth. They eye the movement of his Adam's apple when he swallows saliva and the hair on his chest peeping out between the shirt-buttons of his white shirt. They listen to his soft, almost hoarse voice, as if he needs to clear his throat out now and then.

'…women have two functions: the productive and reproductive,' he says in conclusion. 'It's women who go to educational talks on STDs. Because women are and always have been more tolerant, more intelligent and more open than we men.'

With these final words, he bows his head to applause and bravos. The Mayoress puts her hand on his shoulder to communicate her silent approval.

'If we can lower the shutters a bit and dim the lights…' the tufted aid-worker requests, who has just jumped to his feet.

The shutters function with a crank that opens and shuts, but the Euterpe in charge uses a screwdriver. Once the room is in darkness, he starts to talk. A lady in the third row begins to doze off. The two next to her yawn. Two more leave and a third soon follows.

'Although the African woman has nothing,' the aid-worker relates, 'she does all she can to welcome guests, and it is a mark of disrespect to turn this down. Hospitality is part of her culture. So I will begin by showing you the welcome party they gave us.'

He shows lots of slides of African women smiling, African women carrying plastic washing-up bowls on their heads, animals drinking water from a river and sunsets against a backcloth of trees.

'It is a culture that teaches you to relativise the idea of "the navel of the world" we white Europeans have. Obviously, in Africa, if a person faints on the road, someone will offer them water. In contrast, here, where we are so civilised, between inverted commas, if, for example, let's imagine, one of us here in this room fainted, would anybody here rush to help? Please be honest now…'

'If it was him, I would!' the punk shouts, staring meaningfully at the fair-haired aid-worker. And the other women burst out laughing. As a joke, he acts as if he has passed out, and the Mayoress, quite spontaneously, takes off her plastic ring and puts it in her mouth. She shapes her tongue into an O and puts the tip of her tongue through the ring. Then she craves silence and they all focus on the screen. Now the tufted aid-worker lingers on a slide where a lot of girls are sitting on the ground and waving one arm in the air.

'The girls are at a school, which is one of our projects. Know why they have their hands up?' He pauses. 'They have their hands up because we asked how many went to work after school…! As you can see, the majority do.'

For ten minutes he shows images of babies in hospital and mothers combing their daughters' hair. He puts in a second drum of slides. For another ten minutes he shows images of more animals drinking water and reddish skies until he stops on the picture of a little girl carrying a log on the back of her neck.

'How cute!' the audience exclaims.

'What can you see in this slide?'

'A little girl,' they chorus obediently.

'What do you think the log she is carrying represents?'

'That there's no wood in Africa?' ventures Enriqueta Borrull.

He shakes his head understandingly: 'The little girl is playing. We think it's simply a piece of wood. She thinks it's… her doll. I feel that…' his voice knots, 'this image, for me, sums up Guinea.' He wipes his eyes. 'I'm sorry…'

They all clap again and the noise stirs those who were napping. When the Euterpe in charge switches the light on, six people are in the act of getting up to leave.

'Sorry,' they apologise. 'The fact is…'

'Well now,' the Mayoress continues, 'a few more slides, but this time from Afghanistan, where women don't suffer discrimination. They suffer double discrimination.'

She introduces the aid-worker and asks her to be brief.

'As we have so very little time, all I can really do is sketch in the situation of women in Afghanistan,' she complains as she takes her watch off and puts it on the table. '*I was told* I would have half an hour to forty-five minutes to speak.'

The Mayoress grabs the microphone back: '*You must* understand that the women in our audience unfortunately have to continue working when they get back home. It's their double working-day...'

She nods and looks deadpan. She loads her slides into the projector and looks for a focus to wind out. The tufted aid-worker gets up to help her.

'It's an auto-focus,' he explains.

The Euterpe responsible switches the lights off and the aid-worker starts showing slides where they can see her, with a blue scarf round her head, at a party.

'Afghan women have nothing because, as you know, they have suffered a *non-civil* war (I'm very sorry but I refuse to say that *any* war is civil), but they do all they can to give a special welcome to their guests and it is very rude not to accept. Hospitality is fundamental to Arab culture.'

For ten minutes she shows slides of women drinking tea, sitting on the floor inside their houses.

'This is Shela...' she mutters, as if she were speaking to herself, 'this is Behat... I am still in contact with all these women. In other words I feel a fantastically strong attachment to Kabul. As my colleague put it so well, we think we are "the navel of the world." I felt envious of their collective spirit. Here in the West, cutthroat individualism is the rule. We don't even know our neighbours. But for them it's "I help you, you help me and we'll get by."'

People in the audience are talking about their own things.

'I envied the courage of these women who, in defiance of the regime, gave classes or looked after the sick. And I'd tell them: 'How brave you are and what a coward I am.'

'Shush,' says the security guard. And in an attempt to silence the women at the back, asks to speak: 'OK. How long were you working there?'

'We were there just thirty-five days, but they were incredibly intense. Lived to the max.'

She shows images of the airport, traffic signs and flocks of lambs. And does so in a great rush, as if she doesn't want us to see them. As if they were private and she'd brought them here by mistake. She lingers on a group of little girls with raised arms.

'I won't dwell on this because our colleague has already touched slightly on what I wanted to explain. I suppose you know why these little girls are lifting their arms.

'Because… they work after school?' the women in the front row chorus.

'Spot on. These little girls make rugs. Their rug culture is mega, mega- important. What I'd really like to do now is to give you a snapshot of the culture of the burqa.'

The Euterpe at the table shifts uneasily in her chair. The Mayoress taps the face of her watch twice with her index finger, indicating she's hardly any time left.

'Well, there are *quite a few things* I must sum up in such a short time, you know? The burqa. Well, this burqa thingy that gets us so worked up… This burqa that's become *the* burning political issue… You know, the burqa was originally worn by high-class women! It was a sign of distinction! They'd say: 'Please, Magda, before we resolve the problem of the burqa, we have lots of other priorities.' The burqa is sixth or seventh on their list. But let's proceed. I'll skip the pictures where you'll see how a Westerner like me tried to live for a day wearing a burqa, which are not really that important.'

She quickly shows a series of slides of herself crossing a street wearing a burqa. She stops on the shot of a little boy lying on the ground pushing a slipper with one hand.

'Ah well, although my colleague also trod on my patch here – how apt – I'll still ask you the question I'd planned: do you know what this shoe stands for?'

'A toy,' responds the bored security guard. The punk

stretches her arms and springs back to life.

'Yes, a toy,' she declares. 'For us it's only a shoe. For him, it's a lorry… Could be a lorry carrying humanitarian aid…? I don't know. I leave that on the table.'

Euterpe Manoli slaps herself on her wrist.

'I don't know. There are so many issues I wanted to raise.' She smiles as she reminisces. 'Like for example how I was personally quite surprised that when I asked them about the culture of the harem and bigamy, they really, really lost it with me. They said I was the typically highly ignorant foreign female. You then discover there are highly active women in Arab stories with a great sense of humour. Like in the story of Scheherazade. Any of you familiar with the story of Scheherazade?

The Mayoress grabs the microphone again: 'I think this has been really fascinating and that, in any case, at the end, if we have time…'

The aid-worker presses her lips together and sits down. The Euterpe responsible switches the lights on, and the women in the audience, except for the punk and the Euterpes, leave.

'So sorry,' they apologise.

'It's the double working day,' Enriqueta Borrull laments.

Euterpe Manoli wipes her eyes and takes a cardboard box out from under the table: 'Well, let's proceed to the Women's Prizes for fostering equality,' she announces. She reads out the names of the three winning organizations, and the punk, the Mayoress and the Euterpe women applaud. She hands each representative of the winners a statue of Euterpe the muse and a lilac T-shirt that proclaims: 'Proud to be a woman.'

'We hand-painted them ourselves,' says Enriqueta Borrull. 'Of course, add salt to the first wash, so the ink doesn't run.'

'Thanks on behalf of Afghanistan,' says Carmona the

aid-worker. The tufted aid-worker takes his and puts it over the one he's wearing, without saying a word.

'And, to finish up, there's a bite to eat and a hop!' exclaims Enriqueta Borrull.

Arab music strikes up. The woman in uniform starts filling the glasses with coke and opening bags of crisps and biscuits. The punk goes over to the fair-haired speaker to get him to autograph the handout, but he's already dancing with the Mayoress. Carmona the aid-worker is putting her slides away:

'They force you to come, waste your time and…' she whinges to the tufted aid-worker.

He smiles: 'Do you want to dance, or…?' he gestures.

'Gosh,' she sighs. 'After all I lived through in Afghanistan, I still feel rather out of that scene, I've got a mega-block when it comes to dancing with men. Sorry, right?'

He glances at the fair-haired speaker and the Mayoress who are now imitating belly-dancers gyrating: 'I suppose office work is the solution if you want to live a normal life. Because things can't get to you. From here, the theory seems much more beautiful.'

'Yes.'

'Although I've been lucky, because Guinea, you know, is a fantastically liberated place. The women really exploit their femininity; they possess a sensuality and freedom that *few* women here have. I reckon I've totally taken on board their African freedom and frankness in expressing desire and how you relate to your own body. As they say in Guinea: "Let your heart speak through your body, your body speak through your heart."' She touches an amulet she's wearing round her neck and tears begin to well up again.

No longer such a cold fish she nods and lies on the floor. He does too.

'Take a chair!' the uniformed Euterpe instructs them, as if playfully scolding them.

'No, thanks,' he replies. And he signals to Carmona the

aid-worker to listen carefully, as if wanting to share a secret: 'After you've lived somewhere where the culture of sitting on the floor is so powerful, don't you think *chairs* are fantastically uncomfortable and odd?'

'Gosh,' she sways her head as if she can't believe her ears. 'And how.'

Then squeezes his arm to show just how much she gets his drift.

The Poor Quality of Contemporary Poetry

So he could write *Provincial Lover,* Eladi Susaeta had to ask for six months leave from the private university where he directs the Masters in Journalism. It was the first time he'd ever done such a thing. Two or three weeks had always been enough to put his books together. The words flowed. He finished *The Emperor's Got No Clothes*, a critique of the mediocrity of contemporary literature, in twenty days. *Against Nationalism and Other 'Isms'* took longer, but was in diary form. He polished off *The Alchemist of the Stove*, his gastronomic tour of chef Carlo Puig's life over a long Easter weekend. But *Provincial Lover* was something else. It was the biggest challenge Susaeta had ever faced. 'We decided on you because you write in a more modern, progressive mode, you represent the new Barcelona, the Barcelona that's not stuck in a rut, that doesn't look to the past, but to the future,' said the man from the Town Hall who commissioned him. 'We want you to apply the theories from *The Emperor's Got No Clothes* to this task.' And he couldn't say no.

Provincial Lover will be the words of a song for a publicity clip to promote Barcelona during the World Encounter of Heads of State. El Chaco, the flamenco artiste, will be the singer. And the text will be overlaid with a Garolera drawing. The ad will be placed on television channels and in daily newspapers throughout Europe, the United States and Japan. Susaeta reckons he'll have more readers in a single day than for his whole work in a lifetime. Consequently, he hasn't spent his leave tasting wines in wineries, initiating new polemics on the radio or trying to seduce students on the Masters. He's devoted every waking moment to *Provincial Lover*.

He pours himself a whisky, shuts his office door so the cleaning-lady can't hear him and recites aloud the fruit of all that effort:

> *Provincial Lover*
> I leave my – unassumin' –
> scribblin'.
> The little money I've left
> and my books, by
> my glass of whisky.
>
> Above all, flamenco.
>
> I leave the CDs
> of this immigrant,
> a right-on gal,
> not into nationalisms.
> I'm a dago jumpin' ship,
> but you, kid,
> stay put,
> Yeah, stay put.

In his unassuming opinion, he thinks it's perfect. He puts it in the folder where he keeps his manuscripts and feeds it on to his computer from memory. He then prints four copies. One for his ex-wife, one for his literary agent – who is also his lover –, one for Àngel Gafarró, the journalist, and another for Maribel, a divorcée, who's signed up for the Masters and who, if things go to plan, he can seduce after the campaign is launched.

He first rings his ex-wife. He tells her he's finished it and would like her opinion before handing it over to the press office at the Town Hall. He does this, because although his ex usually reviews his books critically and contemptuously, he finds that, in its way, her judgement is sound. For example, when she read the galleys of *Against Nationalisms and Other 'Isms,'* she spotted a mistake: it wasn't Eisenhower who'd said 'one death is a tragedy and a thousand a statistic,' it was Churchill. But his ex apologises. She's swamped at work and can't make lunch.

'Read it to me over the phone. It can't be that long.'

'I don't think I can read it over the phone, Agnès.' Susaeta is upset she doesn't want to hold it in her hands.

'All right, bring it with you to the bookshop this afternoon.'

He's even more put out at having to go to his ex's bookshop, but agrees to. He phones Maribel and tells her the same story: that he's finished. It turns out she can't make lunch either. She can't leave work till four, so they agree he'll lunch by himself at El Alambique, chef Carlo Puig's restaurant, and she'll drop by for coffee.

She arrives when Susaeta is still scouring his square dessert plate: 'I'm so thrilled…' she says, her eyes glinting. 'It'll be the first original I've ever read. Who else have you shown it to?'

'I wanted you to be the first. I'll only give it to my ex-wife if you give it the go ahead. Then later on I'll call in on my agent for a moment and on a journalist I'm in a love-hate relationship with.' As she doesn't laugh, he adds: 'We're the closest of enemies.'

Maribel sucks her thumb flirtatiously: 'But I don't know how to say interesting things like your agent. And I'm not as sharp-eyed as your ex. I'm a very ordinary reader… I'll disappoint you.'

Susaeta wants Maribel's opinion above all so he can bed her, but also, because out of the three, she's his most loyal reader. Anna-Maria, his agent, is coldly professional, like a rather tiresome, bossy governess, or whatever.

'I want you to tell me "it's got rhythm" or "it hasn't" or "this works, this doesn't". It's a song that could be a poem, and can be read more than one way, do you see? I know I may have got it wrong, because I'm leaping in the dark. It goes way beyond why it's being commissioned. It's not soft on the powers-that-be (if they wanted a text that's soft on power, they chose the wrong person). It's not the classic "Come to Barcelona". It's a dago's view. It's quite a disturbing read.'

All a-tremble, Maribel puts her glasses on and takes the sheet of paper. In the meantime, Susaeta orders a whisky and a cigar. He sees her reading it slowly, reverentially.

'Eladi…' she sighs as she finishes reading. 'Look!' and she shows him her forearm, so he can see she's gone all goose-pimply.

'Do you like it?'

'Oh, immensely. But now I'll play devil's advocate, right? But they're only my silly little thoughts.'

He smiles at her to spur her on to say more but is annoyed when she does decide to share 'her silly little thoughts'.

'First of all: the final sentence. I'd leave it out. It's unnecessary. The song's clear enough without it and I'd say much more dramatic.'

Susaeta wonders whether perhaps she's right. The last sentence is repetitive. Perhaps it doesn't really add anything. Writing is about knowing how to stop in time. Not wanting to tell it all. A poem is like a male orgasm. The climax is in the last line.

'And then, and it's only my intuition, if you like, the glass of whisky.'

'What about the whisky?' Maribel gets his goat occasionally.

'How can I put it?'

He's getting irritated. He's shown her the poem to give her a thrill. Not for her to write a doctoral thesis.

'I find the whisky is a touch facile. As if it was the first thing that came into your head. Of course, it wasn't! I bet you gave it a lot of thought. I bet you know why you put whisky. But you know me, I read everything looking for double meanings, the whys and the wherefores... And I feel whisky is perhaps a touch too... I don't know. The word any hack would use. I'm not explaining myself very well, am I?'

'There's no hidden meaning or logic,' he responds. 'I happen to drink whisky. I'm drinking some right now.' He selects a cigar from those the waiter's offering him.

'Sure, don't take any notice of me. It's like the flamenco bit. I think bringing flamenco in is rather clichéd, as if that was also the first word that came into your head. All the same, you know it's only my reaction and my wanting perfection.'

He nods but really wants to talk about something else. This is what you get for accepting divorcées on your Masters. They start using criteria that are caricatures of the ones you teach them. He's the one that spends his whole time telling them what they write is clichéd and simple-minded. They mustn't write like the hacks hamming it on television. They must find an individual voice. And now she finds clichés everywhere, just to strike a pose. In whatever he does.

'Maybe I could change whisky and put gin, I don't know,' he says to please her. It could be any drink really.

'Yes! That's a great idea!'

As she seems so definite, he puts a line through 'whisky' and writes 'gin'. He reads it aloud:

I leave my – unassumin' –
scribblin'.
The little money I've left
and my books, by
my glass of gin.

'That's perfect!' she enthuses. 'Can you see that?'

'A two-syllable word would fit better. Perhaps I could

put "cognac"?'

'Eladi…' She pauses. 'It *is* cognac. It just *has to be* cognac.'

'Yes. Cognac, perhaps.'

'Like "flamenco". I feel "flamenco" is such a cliché… I'd prefer a musical idiom that was less obvious. I don't know why. Perhaps I've always been rather anti-clichés.'

'Right. I know.'

'As for the title, I wouldn't give the song a title. There's no need to explain what it means as if it were abstract art.'

He closes his eyes as if deep in meditation. The idea appeals.

'You know, I could delete the title. You're right.'

'I love you so much! You're my genius! Fantastically talented!' She takes her glasses off and bows her head, as if shocked by her own temerity. She puts the tip of her little finger up to her right eye and wipes away an incipient tear, and, in the process, opens her mouth quite unconsciously: 'And what about the last sentence, Eladi? I reckon you should give it another whirl. I'm absolutely sure you don't need it.'

He nods, half convinced. And to prove it, crosses it out and reads:

I leave the CDs
of this immigrant,
a right-on gal,
not into nationalisms.
I'm a dago jumpin' ship,
but you, kid,
stay put.

'Do you see now, Eladi? It's a thousand times more dramatic.'

He strokes her cheek and reminds her he must be off now to show the song to his ex-wife. Maribel thinks that's perfectly OK, but she's sore. Her period ended five days ago and now was the ideal moment to go to bed with Susaeta for the first time, and not use a condom. She's not been to bed with anyone since she divorced and reckons he's not a man to notice whether women have flab hanging from their arms or sagging breasts, but one to appreciate their sense of humour and intellect. She's jealous of his ex.

'Give some thought to the flamenco, right?'

He signals to the waiter to bring him the bill by scribbling in the air with his right hand. The waiter waves the palms of his hands, as if blocking the way, meaning, for God's sake, this is on the house. And Susaeta raises his arms to the heavens to indicate he's shocked. Maribel seems rather too overwhelmed by the scene, seemingly a well-rehearsed ritual, until the attendant brings them their coats ands helps put them on. They walk out into the street and say goodbye. Susaeta kisses her hand, says thank you and they go off in opposite directions. She's off to take the metro. He stops a taxi, and uses the journey to write out clean copy.

When he gets to the bookshop he finds his ex and her business partner barefoot hanging globes and papier-mâché moons in the shop window. She immediately stops. Puts her shoes on and asks him for his text.

'But I'll have to read it in the office, because I get nervous when you're watching me,' she warns. 'I'll give you a shout.'

To while the time away Susaeta browses between the shelves and notices that *Stop the World, I'm Getting Off*, the collection of articles by journalist Marga Bel is no longer on the table of new publications and it's only been on sale two days. What she deserves, thinks Susaeta. She's superficial and always writing about what she does in the gym with her gay friends. His Masters students know he can't stand her. However, there's another compilation of articles in the window and on the bestseller table: *Don't Shoot the Journalist*, by Martí Campos, a shyster, a student of his from last year whom he's hated ever since. He had a high opinion of himself just because he wrote about hip-hop and service stations. He also saw himself as a disciple of Àngel Gafarró, rather than of himself. Susaeta failed him. He didn't deserve to pass. Now he writes a regular column in a daily paper. Even Anna-Maria reckons his writing is 'a breath of fresh air'.

Susaeta surreptitiously grabs *Smooth Thighs*, the novel that won the last *Femina* prize, and hides the pile of Campos's books. His ex shouts: 'Eladi!'

When he walks into her office, the first thing he sees on top of her desk is his text full of scrawls, crossings out, question and exclamation marks in red. He feels like he's been raped.

'Shall we have a word then, Eladi?'

'Yes, let's.' These mysterious airs of hers infuriated him. Why doesn't she come out and say whether she likes it or not, and cut the prima donna bit?

'How about a drink?'

'Can't we get it over with now? I've got an appointment with Anna-Maria. I can't cancel it.' He doesn't say Anna-Maria is his lover because she'd turn jealous.

'Just as you like.' Susaeta can see she's offended.

'I did want to have lunch with you, if you remember.'

'Yes.'

'Why don't we do something special tomorrow?' he suggests, trying to fix something. 'Shall I reserve a table at El Alambique?'

'Let's wait on that. It was OK to scrawl on the paper, wasn't it?'

'Yes, of course,' he responds as casually as he knows how. 'It's a working copy.'

His ex says that in principle she likes the song, but would eliminate the last sentence. It's unnecessary. It's clear enough without it, and much more to the point. It's surely easy on the eye. But, what does it add in fact? Isn't it mere padding? If he cut it out, wouldn't the text seem much more austere? And not to mention the letters 'CD' that she finds a facile concession to the trendies. He starts with 'CD' and ends on 'hip-hop,' quite à la Martí Campos.

Susaeta ponders and thinks she's right. He knows she'll now start to tell him he talks too glowingly about the 'right-on girl'. She always finds something to 'but' about the women who appear in his books.

'Perhaps you're right.' He takes a pen out of his shirt pocket and makes some changes. He reads the final section aloud to see how it sounds:

> I leave the VINYLS
> of this immigrant,
> a right-on gal,
> not into nationalisms.
> I'm a dago jumpin' ship,
> but you, kid,
> stay put.

It's true it's now less obvious, Susaeta concurs. It's as if the poet is asking Barcelona to stay put. Perhaps.

'Perhaps you're right.'

'You do what you want, but it's as clear as daylight to me.' She gathers momentum: 'I also think the phrase about the "right-on gal" is rather playing to the gallery.'

'It's the heart and soul of the poem. I can't eliminate that.'

'You can't? That's your business. As far as I am concerned, the "immigrant" and "gal" rhyme is really poor.' He looks half persuaded.

He bids farewell to his ex and jumps into another taxi. Heads off to Anna-Maria's literary agency, a loft in the Born district, he writes clean copy with the latest corrections. Gives it another read before ringing the bell, and then walks upstairs.

He'd not met up with Ann-Maria during his leave, but just before it they'd entered the stage in their relationship when both were beginning to feel bored. Going out to eat or to bed had lost the charm of novelty. They did both but less often or enthusiastically. What most depressed him about the boredom was the fact she too was bored. Physically Anna-Maria's like all the literary agents he knows: thin, short and flat-chested. She also dresses like all the others: garishly.

'You brought it with you?' she asked.

They hug each other and he nods.

'Who else you shown it to?'

'To Agnès. I'll also show it to Àngel Gafarró.'

He doesn't mention any divorcée Masters student because he suspects she'll immediately assume he wants to seduce her.

'A very good idea. Gafa's got *very sound* judgement. More than I have. I probably haven't got much of interest to say. Besides, you know my role is to play devil's advocate.'

While she's reading, Susaeta reviews the photographs of the writers hanging on her wall. There are some new ones. Anna-Maria is all the time taking on more and more authors with big media profiles, and that makes it more difficult for her to represent those with any real quality. One of these days they should have a serious talk.

'Eladi…' Anna-Maria mutters once she's finished.

'What do you think?'

'It's the best you've ever written.'

'So you think it's a strong piece?' he asks unassumingly.

'I do. It would be even stronger if you axed the last sentence. Is that what your ex told you?'

'She said that about a sentence that's no longer there.'

'OK. All right. I understand. That's why it so hangs in the air. The "I'm a dago jumpin' ship" is a terminally weak ending. Conversely, "not into nationalisms" will up the ante.' To underline what's she's saying, she puckers her lips and shakes her forearm with her fist clenched, as if imitating a banger exploding. She's already taken her pen from her pocket.

'I leave the VINYLS
of this immigrant,
a right-on gal
not into nationalisms.'

'What do you think?' she asks contentedly.

'Yes, maybe that's stronger.'

'It's got much more... woomph!' and she repeats her previous gesture. 'As a matter of balance, I'd put "cognac" in capitals: your drink and the right-on gal's vinyls.

'You like the way it doesn't say who it is?'

'I think it's the best and subtlest bit of the song.'

'You surprised it doesn't have a title?'

'It's very spare,' she lies, because she hadn't noticed.

'And does "cognac" work?'

'Let's say: it doesn't bother me. "my scribblin'" bothers me more.'

'In what way?'

'"I leave my scribblin'" sounds rather like a will. It's very journalistic. I reckon it would be enough to leave your money and books. You don't need to leave your writings physically: they're in the library.'

'What would *you* put then?'

'Just leave your money and books. Period. I think that's much more modest. Much more your style.'

'It's hard to say:"I leave the little money I've left, and my unassumin' books".'

'What if you put "notebook"? That's much more unassuming and I think, precisely for that reason, much more brilliant.'

'"Notebook" wouldn't rhyme with "unassumin'".'

'What does "unassumin'" add, Eladi? Tell me, what does it really add?'

'The little money I've left,
and my notebook, next to

67

the glass of COGNAC.

Above all, flamenco.

I leave the VINYLS
of this right-on gal,
not into nationalisms.'

Once he's read it, Susaeta can see she's right. It's an improvement. It's much more minimalist. She's spot on. He thanks her and starts to make a clean copy. If it's fine by her, he thinks they've done what they can and he rushes off to meet Àngel Gafarró. He can't think of anything else until the poster's printed and the ad's recorded, but when this is all over, they'll go back to eat at El Alambique, like before. She nods and smiles. She's pleased he's going. Now, after not seeing him for half a year, she's not panting to go out with him again. Besides, she fancies that radio pundit she likes who's just signed a contract to be represented by her.

Susaeta meets up with Gafarró in a hotel bar in the centre of town. Relations between the two have been lukewarm ever since Susaeta criticised him in *Against Nationalisms and Other 'Isms'*. In revenge Gafarró wrote an article making fun of *The Alchemist of the Stove*, in which he asked whether the owner of the supermarket chain who'd paid for the book knew that it's impossible to find 'a sensual prawn'; not because the jury's out on the sensuality of prawns, but because it's not an ingredient in vegetarian rice. For months Susaeta got nightly calls from someone asking him if he was a fishmonger and sold sensual prawns. He had to get an answering machine. Obviously Susaeta could not show him his text, for risk of getting a ferocious review in the magazine *Ambigú*, where Gafarró writes under a pseudonym.

No sooner have they said their hellos than Gafarró announces he is short of cash and it would be a good idea to eat a cheese and bacon sandwich. Susaeta knows he does this on purpose, so he's forced to say this kind of hotel doesn't do cheese and bacon sandwiches.

'Oh, Susaeta! If only I had all your friends among the powers-that-be and got the jobs you get…!' sighs Gafarró, slapping him on the back. He always acts poverty-stricken with him.

He starts to read, immediately pointing out that cognac isn't drunk from a glass, but maybe as his readers are used to finding all manner of oddities in his books, they won't mind. He also says 'flamenco' and 'cognac' hardly rhyme and that it's rather cynical to say he's leaving 'little money,' when you think what he's been paid to write the song. It would be more honest not to specify the amount. On the other hand, he doesn't think it very logical for him only to leave a notebook, because one can assume he had lots. Nor can he see why he's put a phrase like 'not into nationalisms' at the end of the poem. It's superfluous. He should know how to rein himself in. A much better ending would be 'right-on gal'.

That night, Susaeta shuts himself in his office and re-writes:

'I leave the money I've left,
by my balloon of COGNAC.

Above all, flamenco.

I leave the VINYLS
of this right-on gal.

The following day he gives his end product to Garolera the painter so he can do the illustration. Garolera thinks the song sublime, except for the last line that he personally would leave out.

'Playing devil's advocate, I'd say I don't understand what

this unknown girl is doing ending the song. It's as if the text has two levels. One – the first – is very private. The other's cruder. "Gal" and "right-on" don't go with "by my balloon of cognac."'

Susaeta thinks that's quite true. He goes home, sups on odds and ends, shuts himself in his study, crosses out the last line, and reviews the final result.

I leave the money I've left,
by my balloon of COGNAC.

Above all, flamenco.

It's perfect. Re-writing, re-drafting is the secret of creation. He's decided the next book he'll write will be a critique of the poor quality of contemporary poetry being written in their country. He's already got his opening sentence: 'The first to write "your teeth are pearls" was a genius. The most recent, a fool.'

The next day he lunches at El Alambique with the Town Hall's press officer who gave him the commission. He reads the text over dessert and congratulates him: it's wonderfully condensed. So much so, that he thinks – and it is a humble layman's opinion – that it would be better without 'the money I've left'. Playing devil's advocate, he thinks it's superfluous to repeat that the money is the writer's. Particularly because the song is aimed at people throughout the world and the idea they want to sell is not of a country turned in upon itself, with mean inhabitants obsessed with making money. On the contrary. It should speak of generous, open, Mediterranean people. As for the cognac, anyone's free to drink whatever he wishes, naturally, but what a pity that the narrating 'I' – given he drinks – doesn't drink Catalan wine, cava or, at the very least, a liqueur more typical of the country where he is writing.

'"Cognac" sounds good before "flamenco",' Susaeta

defends himself, 'and I can't put "a glass of cava" if the poem is supposed to be a critique of provincialism!'

Immediately, the official says he understands, and doesn't in any way want to restrict his freedom. But insists he can't mention flamenco in the last line. What's important is that the words are like a will and testament. And a testament for a writer are the money and the balloon. It's taking 'sensitivity too far' to emphasise he's also bequeathing flamenco. Besides, Garolera's painting will explain in the universal language of painting Susaeta's feeling for flamenco. People will understand the sub-text.

He tries it out:

I leave the money here,
by my balloon of COGNAC.

Right then. We now have a song. It explains in a very few words the contradictory love Susaeta feels for the city; a sincere, but critical love. It's finished and that same afternoon, four messengers leave the Town Hall with copies for the composer, the page-maker and the filmmaker who will film the ad and the singer.

Two days later, Susaeta is correcting galleys. He almost has a heart attack when he realises they've put 'cognac' in lower case by mistake. The officer then admits it's too late to correct anything, because he supposed Susaeta wouldn't want to make changes and the text was put to bed hours ago.

'They're a bunch of bureaucrats,' he complains to Anna-Maria, while, kneeling down, her mouth level with his fly, she tries to console him.

An excited Maribel calls him as soon as she receives a copy of her poster and the CD. She thinks the song is beautiful and is very pleased he took her comments on board. She's particularly pleased he decided to put 'cognac' in small case. She'd thought as much when she saw the last draft but hadn't dared say anything. His ex makes no comment.

Reviews come out throughout the week in the different cultural supplements of the daily newspapers. In one, they describe the words as 'a masterpiece' and in another as 'a contemporary, urban haiku written from the outside.' One daily doesn't print a review but a letter to the editor says it's 'a fraud paid for by taxpayers' money.' A comedian on his radio programme says it's 'a leg-pull,' and the man who introduces the only books programme on television (who writes for the paper that didn't publish a review) describes it as 'a joke in bad taste'. Àngel Gafarró, in the magazine *Ambigú*, praises Garolera's painting while regretting the big letters of the text partially obscure it.

Susaeta ensures that neither Anna-Maria nor his ex get invitations to the launch of the campaign. He knows Gafarró won't go, because he has a meeting at the same time at the College of Journalists to protest against the sacking of the woman editor of a radio programme.

On the night of the party, Maribel appears in a long, silvery dress, with matching handbag. It's so small that from a distance Susaeta thinks it's a baguette wrapped in foil. Maribel is such a character. He's relieved to see his eyes are playing tricks on him.

'*Tu sei così bella…*' he whispers. And kisses the tips of her fingers.

The event starts. After the mayor's speech, Garolera, the composer and the director of the ad speak. Finally, it's his turn: 'If you don't mind, as ever, I will let my words speak for me,' and he then recites:

I leave the money here,
by my balloon of cognac.

The audience applauds rapturously. Then, the French translator of the text, who's the next to climb on the stage, gives his thanks for the grant he received for his work and explains the difficulties he found in transforming Susaeta's singular musicality into the language of Molière without losing the power of the original. (Particularly when working in such a rush). He puts his glasses on and reads:

Je laisse l'argent ici,
À côté du ballon de cognac.

The translators into Italian, Galician, English, Basque and two translators into Japanese also read their versions of the words. Someone switches the lights out and the images of the ad are projected on the cinema screen. You can see Gaudí's La Pedrera, the Sagrada Familia and an aerial view of the city. El Chaco appears barefoot on the steps up to the Parc Güell. The guitarist plays two chords, and sings: 'I leave the money here, by my balloon of cognac…' He shrieks the end: '… of cognac.'

More applause follows and one or two 'bravos'. The lights go up and drinks are served.

'Can you do me a favour?' Maribel asks Susaeta in an aside. 'Can you give me the original text as a present and autograph it?' Her eyes dampen.

He caresses her arm: 'I've got it at home. If you like, we can go for a last shot of whisky and I'll give it you there.'

She agrees to this as she wipes away her tears. She had her period a fortnight ago so now they'll be forced to use a condom, but she imagines he'll have some around the house. It's obvious they're deserting the party – but in fact nobody notices – and they grab a taxi. They maul each other on the journey, but not overly, because she acts as if she's embarrassed. When they get to his flat, she asks where the bathroom is. Susaeta uses this time to write the words on a cream-coloured sheet of paper. When she comes out, he gives it to her.

'The date?'

Susaeta puts the date on.

'I'll get this framed,' she says and so she doesn't forget it puts it with all the care in the world on the table in the entrance hall.

They snog on the sofa. Maribel unties Susaeta's musketeer's locks – he'd tied them in a ponytail – and her hands are so sticky with hair-cream she has to wipe them surreptitiously on the pillow. As they don't have any condoms, she gives him a session of oral sex that Susaeta rates worse than Anna-Maria's and better than Agnès's, and he gives her an equivalent suck, that Maribel can't compare, because it's her first ever.

In deep embrace, they talk about the French version of the song, perhaps because the translator is truly mediocre and has worked over confidently and lost the power of the original. She should have checked with the author over her doubts. They also complain about the resentment expressed by some of Susaeta's professional colleagues. They conclude that nowhere else in the world do people who devote themselves to writing bear these grudges, rather than rallying round. But it's time for the gossip programme on Channel Three and they decide to take a look. They feel that the fact they watch this programme, and not their previous sex, ratifies the start of their relationship. They go to bed and sleep in a 4/4 formation.

In the morning, she gets up at seven because she'd rather have a shower at home and change her clothes before going to work. They agree to dine at El Alambique. Susaeta starts to stir at around eight, and at nine he goes to the newspaper library to collect information for his book on the poor quality of contemporary poetry (he wants to have it ready in a couple of weeks). He doesn't notice, in all the commotion, that Maribel left the words behind. The cleaning lady does find them at eleven when she goes to clean his flat. She puts on her glasses and reads. Intrigued, she looks on the table. Ah, that peculiar Mr Susaeta. She can't see a glass of cognac anywhere. And where the hell did he leave the money?

Letter to My
Non-Biological Child

'Don't worry, we won't eat anyone,' says the grey-haired psychologist.

And we all laugh we're so nervous. There are four psychologists spread around the four corners of the meeting room mingling with us. I'm not sure if it's a strategic decision or pure chance. This is an obligatory meeting and will last all of today, Friday and all of Saturday, under the rubric 'Approach Routes and Preparations for Adoption'. The purpose is to help them decide if we are suitable adoptive parents.

I scrutinise the other women. And it's strange to think they must all have had sex with their men trying to get pregnant; women beneath and men on top, to facilitate the spermatozoons' penetration. I imagine them with their feet up on the headboard, at the end, so the semen slips deep down and I also imagine them crying when their period starts. They'll have talked and talked: today's good, no point today, I'm not fertile.

'We will start this morning by getting to know each other, expressing our doubts, doing role-play... Tomorrow some adoptive parents will drop in and give us a presentation, and finally we will hold the individual interviews,' explains the grey-haired psychologist.

When she hears her mention individual interviews, one of the participants shudders, and everyone laughs again.

'We want to discuss briefly with you the reasons why you've chosen the route of adoption.'

The psychologist who said this slurps her tongue all the time like a girl eating a sweet. She's the best-looking. Her legs are so smooth and dark that, at first glance, I don't register she's not wearing tights; she's even got a white, oblong scar on her knee, shaped like the flat variety of toothpick and looking like the start of a ladder. She also tells us what the foundation for which they work is called and says the headquarters of their foundation is in this hospital, but that it's got nothing to do with the hospital, it just loans us the room. In no way must we feel we are in a hospital, she stresses.

'Don't worry, we're not going to eat you,' the grey-haired lady repeats.

'So no interrogation today?' my guy asks, jokingly. And he takes out his pen (the one I gave him as a present) and notebook from his briefcase.

'It's *not* an interrogation,' the leggy psychologist corrects him.

The third psychologist, sitting in the right-hand corner, suggests everyone give a short bio to start the ball rolling: 'Say, for example, you?' She points to the first couple, 'Who are you? What are your expectations from the course? And why do you want to adopt?'

The woman explains her name is Magda Carreras and that she works as a journalist (that's when I recognise her: she's half famous). Her husband already has two biological daughters from a previous marriage and they have decided that now it would be right to adopt a third child.

'It's Magda Carreras, your mate,' I whisper to my guy, because he always switches channel when he sees her on the television.

'Only just noticed? I spotted her hours ago.'

Then it's the turn of a tall woman who's come by herself. She's a primary schoolteacher and wants to adopt a Chinese girl. (She says, 'A Chinky girl'.) The grey-haired woman immediately asks her if she's given up the idea of living as a couple.

'No, not at all. I'm really up for having a partner, but I don't want to wait anymore to become a mother, because I've got to an age…' she recites, as if she'd learned this off by heart before coming.

She's wearing flat, laced shoes, jeans and a check shirt. I keep nodding in support of her. I have the feeling she is a lesbian and doesn't want the psychologists to rumble her. Next it's the turn of a married couple who work as music teachers. He has a black, curly beard; she's got long, untidy hair held in place by a tiara. They both speak very slowly and, whenever they hear a noise – a door banging or an ambulance's distant sirens – they shut their eyes and their faces freeze in a painful grimace. They tried artificial insemination, they say, but it didn't work. This had made them reflect that Nature, in her wisdom, by not giving them the child they were hoping for, was sending out a message. The message that perhaps they should adopt. The other couple run a 99 cent shop, and are already parents of a fifteen-year old girl and twelve-year old boy: 'But we've done temporary care three times and it's a very enriching experience,' he explains. 'I've put up a web-page where we describe it, now and then, all plain and matter-of-fact.'

His wife adds that they want a child from Nepal because someone on their estate has already adopted a boy from there. When they hear this, Magda Carreras and my guy, who are sitting next to each other, exchange words, and look quite shocked.

'What were you saying?' I ask.

'That the reason for wanting a child from Nepal is a bit off. This isn't a supermarket for children!' He's very annoyed and likes people to notice.

'Miquel?' the fourth psychologist addresses him.

'Well, I serve my time *perpetrating* scripts for the cultural section on the Midday News. You know what being the culture bit on the news implies. Well, rather than write scripts, our task is to get past the censure, in inverted commas. He outlines these with his index and middle finger. As per usual.

The psychologist smiles and looks at me.

'I work as a telephonist,' I say. 'Or rather saleswoman for a telephone company.' I swallow saliva. 'We've thought a lot about adopting.'

'Ours is a very considered decision,' adds Miquel straightaway. 'A good way to re-adjust North–South inequalities is for the North not to have children and adopt them from the South.'

'But are you able to have children?' continues the psychologist. She's a real nosey-parker.

'We don't know,' Miquel affirms complacently. 'That doesn't concern us one iota.'

'Are you thinking of having biological children?'

'Why not? But later on, maybe.'

I look at the ground. We don't fuck anymore, but that isn't something the psychologists need to know. I'm worried we might be the only ones doing this course that won't get the certificate.

We set to. The fourth psychologist, by the name of Eutalia, explains that to start with we'll make a list on the whiteboard of the children's positives and drawbacks and, then, those of the parents. She draws a green line down the middle of the board. On the left she writes 'Positives,' on the right, 'Drawbacks'. She underlines the words and airily asks everyone to volunteer their ideas.

'Well? Shall I break the ice?' my guy asks me. Before I've had time to reply he's in full swing: 'Drawback? He's not known love. Positive? He's got lots to give you.'

Everyone smiles, visibly very moved, and he presses his lips together in a self-satisfied smile. Last night he was surfing the web on suitability courses, to find out what they'd be asking.

'Come on, more things,' the grey-haired psychologist

urges. 'Please do understand we're not doing it to try to catch you out.' Those words 'catch out' aren't ones I'd ever imagine a psychologist using.

'Could one drawback be that we don't speak the same language?' asks Magda Carreras, her voice emotionally strangled.

'And a positive, that children have a fantastic aptitude for languages,' adds Miquel.

The psychologist nods, but she doesn't write anything down. To encourage those who have yet to speak, she explains that one drawback the child feels is fear of a second rejection. 'Fears rejection,' she writes.

By midday, the whiteboard is full of drawbacks and positives and they give us a half-hour break.

'Who's up for sandwiches and coffee?' Miquel asks.

The all for 99 cents pair are, as well as the couple who speak very, very slowly. The single woman picks up her bag and blouson and says nothing.

'I've got to catch up on the news,' the Carreras woman says, opting out.

'Come on, it will help to get to know each other,' Miquel insists. 'There's a café downstairs.' I can see that he's disappointed she's not coming. He now wants to be one of those staying put.

'Why you hanging back?' I nag him when nobody's listening. 'You're sucking up to her. You say you don't like her and all you do is follow her like a lap-dog.'

'I don't like her. I'm making fun of her. Can't you see that?'

I grab my jacket and smile, and don't answer. As I'm afraid the psychologists will see we're arguing, I smile non-stop.

'Oh, all right then,' sighs Carreras, as if she's had second thoughts. 'I need a double espresso.'

Right on: she's the kind of woman who *needs* things. A double espresso, a smoke, a shot, to disconnect, relax, put order in her life.

She talks non-stop in the bar. She says her publishers have suggested she write a book on adoption, in the form of a letter to her son or daughter, and she's agreed. It will be called, *Letter to My Non-biological Child*. It will be quite short, but to the point, with photos illustrating the whole process. She's accepted the commission because she wants to explain that adoption, unlike biological paternity, is really a labour pain that parents share fifty-fifty.

Miquel has been chewing his nails for some time. He asks for the bill and divides it up: 'The bad news is that it's seven euros a couple or three and a half per person. That's including a tip.' And while everyone is getting out their five or ten euro notes, he adds, 'It's compulsory in the United States. Once the whole crew from the telly flew there for a congress…'

He tells a story he always tells about a bar in New York, but the music teachers are talking to the single woman about possible countries to adopt from, and everyone is listening to them.

'We want him or her to be like us as much as is possible,' the husband is explaining. 'Not because we're selfish but because there's still so much racism in society today…'

When he finds an opening, Miquel announces he too has been asked to write a book on adoption, but in a humorous vein.

'If you'd like me to give it a look over…' the Carreras woman chimes in condescendingly. 'I'll give it a glance and mark things up…'

He nods ingratiatingly. He moves his lips and repeats – absolutely silently – what she's just said. It's one of his tics. He does it when he's watching telly or arguing with me. His lips pucker like a fish, as if he were perplexed and can't work out what's happening. In our early days together he'd make me laugh when he did this and I always poked fun at him.

'Shall we go back up?' he shouts. 'Our carers must be

getting worried.' I kiss him on the arm.

We find the psychologists still separating out the chairs. Right away, the one called Eulàlia explains it's time for the role-play. We must divide into teams. The scene will be one couple inviting other couples to dinner to tell them they've been allotted a thirty-month old baby from Romania. One of the couples thinks this isn't a good idea, the other does.

'It's not obligatory,' the leggy psychologist explains. 'We don't want to force you to do anything, but it's a very good way to get rid of gremlins and doubts and reproduce the situation you'll all find yourselves in.'

We look at each other and don't know what to do until Carreras gets up:

'Fine, I'm up for it.'

'Excellent!' the one by the name of Eulàlia congratulates her. And looks at her husband, 'You plucking up courage as well, Manel?'

'I'm quite embarrassed.'

'I'd like you all to take part. But we're not into forcing people.'

Miquel lifts a hand: 'Go on, I'll join in.'

'What about you?' she turns to me.

'I don't act at all well.'

'No, no, no,' she chides me. 'It's not about being an actor. I want us to be very clear about this. It's a game. It's role-playing.'

The all for 99 cents stand up.

'We need two more,' the woman by the name of Eulàlia reminds the music teachers. And they get up. The single woman, Mr Carreras and I look at each other.

'Come on then, let's assign roles,' says the leggy one. 'Who are going to be the ones who've adopted the child?'

And the all for 99 cents man waves his index finger.

'Anyone feel like being the one against?'

'Ok, me,' says Mrs Carreras. And she says it so decisively everyone laughs, licking their lips in anticipation.

'Can I be your husband?' asks Miquel, dramatically. I feel jealous. I watch them happily link arms.

'Very well, we'll be the ones who are for,' the music teacher suggests. Meanwhile, Mrs Carreras and Miquel, in a corner, whisper ideas to each other, as if they were preparing their role-play.

'We'll be with you anon!' he proclaims. And they go into the corridor. The psychologists sway their heads approvingly. It's obvious they're pleased there are such good vibrations.

'These chairs and the table are your house, right?' the leggy one reminds the music teachers.

In next to no time, Mrs Carreras and Miquel knock on the door and their entrance makes everyone burst out laughing. She's slung her blouson over her shoulders like an old dame trying to be trendy, and dangles her bag from her wrist. He's wet his hair and swept it back with his hand. They look like the leads from a comic opera.

'Let's begin!' indicates the leggy psychologist, swaying her head. 'But don't over-exaggerate, right?'

The all for 99 cents couple act as if they're cooking. She imitates the movements of someone slicing lettuce on a chopping board and he acts as if he's opening a bottle of wine and filling his wife's glass. He sniffs the cork and sniffs the wine and, from his actions, it must be a tall, wide glass. They make a toast. And seem happy. But it's as if she were making more effort to make a show of it than he is. She hugs him from the back, plays at putting food in his mouth and exclaims: 'Mmm…!' as if what he was preparing is really good. She also taps him on the backside. And sits down on one of the tables (acting as if she'd really sat on a kitchen top). She says: 'Not again, we've forgotten to put some beer in the fridge. We're a real disaster…!'

The psychologists keep giving instructions, as if they were teaching performance: ''Maybe you're afraid your friends don't agree with your decision and you're talking that over?'

'Maybe you're discussing the best way to tell your friends what you've decided?'

Miquel and Mrs Carreras start walking to where you imagine there's a door and, once there, sing 'ding-dong!' as if ringing the bell. 'Hey, how are you? Like a drink? Yes, I'll pour out the wine, as we've good news. What news? Let's see, do sit down: we won't go round the houses. They allocated us a thirty-month old kid from Romania. Adoptive? Yes, adoptive. But it's going to be hard on the adopted kid. He'll be treated like a bricklayer around here.'

The four of them do it so well I shiver in embarrassment. I get goose-pimples. Next to me, Mr Carreras is red with worry and his eyes are glinting. He looks at me and gives me a faint smile, poor guy. I smile back. Then I straighten up and gesture to the leggy psychologist: 'Can I go to the toilet?' I ask her. 'The coffee's coming back at me and I feel terrible.'

'Can't you wait for the game to finish?'

'I feel like being sick.' I don't know why I'm saying this.

'So do I,' whines Mr Carreras. And he puts a hand on his belly. 'I feel out-of-sorts here too.' He grimaces, as if he'd got heart-burn.

'Stop for a minute!' orders the leggy psychologist. 'We've got two people here who don't feel well. Anyone else feel queasy?'

'No,' answers Miquel. 'What's wrong?'

'The milk in the coffee was off,' I make my excuses. 'I thought it tasted funny. I feel like being sick. We feel, I mean.'

'I feel quite normal and I also had a spot of milk,' he replies suspiciously. He's very peeved we've spoiled their performance, that's quite evident.

'I also thought the coffee tasted a bit strange,' the single woman comes to our aid.

'Go on, off to the toilet!' the grey-haired psychologist

rushes us off.

We go out into the passageway and run to the toilet, two doors further down. Once inside, we smile at each other not knowing what to do next.

'We won't get our certificate,' I predict.

The guy laughs nervously.

'My wife will kill me.' But he turns a tap on with great determination and cups his hands. He wets my forehead. Then wets his own. We squat down and lean our heads against the tiled wall. We can hear the performance that's been resumed: 'I don't know why you have to be such lefties,' Miquel complains, hamming away. 'This didn't use to happen *before*!' We hear a ripple of laughter. 'But don't you see that when the maid goes to fetch him from school, people will think he's her son?' argues Mrs Carreras. There's more muttering and his voice again: 'In the area where you live they'll take him for an immigrant!' After a while, the door to the meeting room opens and shuts and we hear a woman's heels tapping towards the toilet.

'They're coming to get us,' the guy warns me. 'We'll say we've been sick.'

I see he's got a very lurid burn mark on his neck, as if he'd been scalded when he was little. I can't tell whether he's thirty or forty-five years old. He's got a big nose – which I like – and a pencil-thin mouth.

The grey-haired psychologist is carrying my bag and the two jackets: 'Hey. Couple? How's it going? How are you?'

'We've been sick,' he says. 'It was the milk. For sure.'

'You'd better go to Casualty. Don't stay in the toilets. Go to Casualty and let them take a look at you.'

We get up, take our things and follow her.

'Don't be worrying now about your suitability. We'll decide later what we'll do with you two. It's nerves, I expect.'

She stops in the doorway and points to the Casualty

department at the other side of the garden.

'Come back, as soon as you feel better, right? We'll see whether we've still time to hear the feedback.'

We nod and start walking slowly clasping our bellies. It's sunny and the man sneezes. It's a curious sneeze. The groan he lets out must be the same as when he ejaculates I reckon. It's a long, lukewarm 'eeh,' a combination of revulsion and despair.

'Nice to be out here,' I say.

'I want a smoke,' says he. 'Do you? You do, don't you?'

I turn round furtively to see whether the psychologist is still in the doorway. She isn't.

'They'll spot the smell.'

But the guy says they won't, sure they won't, they won't smell it at all because we're in the open air, and he sits on a bench and takes out his packet of cigarettes. He says that if they catch us we can give the excuse that we felt queasy and were afraid of being sick in the waiting-room. That we preferred to stay outside and breathe in the fresh air.

I'm not entirely convinced, but I sit down as well. He places two cigarettes in his mouth, lights them and gives me one. It's a gesture I've not seen in years. It reminds me of the time when I used to go clubbing at the age of fifteen or sixteen. I had a boyfriend who was always doing it. He'd put two cigarettes in his mouth, light them up and give the first to me. He always ordered vodkas and orange. I inhale. There are a lot of Japanese in the garden taking photos of the modernist hospital and patients and relatives out for a stroll. The sun is shining. A sickly creature is dragging her bag of serum on an apparatus on wheels. Doctors also walk up and down.

The Annual Evolution of the Human Voice

For the whole of the Christmas party the radio station staff hold in the flat of the night-time presenter, the news editor and comic sketch writer stick cheek by jowl. He's brought 80s music and, living up to her reputation as an uninhibited, extravagant spontaneous type, she never stops dancing. When nobody's watching they go out on the terrace. They introduce themselves: Ernest and Àngels. Two kisses. They've never coincided before because they have different work schedules. They start to chat. How funny we've never met at the station. But it isn't really a coincidence, in fact. Yes, you're right, I mean it's strange, when, on the other hand, we have so much in common. Oh, it is, isn't it?

They sit down on the wicker chairs and she pretends she's cold. He rubs her shoulders and hugs her quite offhandedly. But she's already telling him about the idea for a television script she's thought up. It's a series of monologues on everyday life ('in humorous mode,' she says), but seen from a feminine point of view. Like, say, 'The manufacturers of chocolate want us to have periods.' He laughs and this makes her really happy. (A sense of humour is what she values most in a person.) In order to seduce him, she praises him to the skies listing everything she can't stand about men. He feels both flattered (he likes to be special, mature, shy and seemingly serious as she describes) and in dread (he's probably macho and predictable, something she can't stand), but as he's had a drink or two he finds her pretty and immediately musters up the courage to kiss her. When they disentangle, Àngels puts one hand over her mouth and shakes the other as if she were a kid who's misbehaved. He looks at her enraptured.

'You're a real clown. It is *really* incredible. You're like a child, your little eyes are so naïve…' he coos.

And she opens them as wide as she can, and pouts timidly.

The night after they meet and go to bed. The morning shower and breakfast are no disappointment. By the afternoon they are showing each other their childhood compositions. Day after day there are more joint showers and breakfasts, and each shower, each breakfast confirms they are made for each other. They decide to move in together.

The first two months of cohabitation is pure plain sailing. He tells her she's like a child and she behaves as if she were: whenever she eats cream, she tries to daub her nose in it as if she hasn't noticed; before she puts the eggs in their eggcups, she draws smiles on them with a black felt-tip, and when she's window shopping, she puts her palms on the glass and steams it up. He's continually taking surprise photos of her. He catches her sticking her tongue out or talking to the plants, but above all he captures those girlish eyes. Sometimes, after a photo-session, she gets headaches from the effort it's been to keep them wide open so long. Every day they say how much they love each other and that they'll never be like other couples they know. They promise: they'll desire and love one another forever, even into old age. When they're old, she'll still be a little girl. If one day they decide their love and desire isn't as intense as it is now, they'll finish it there and then, because they could never live with mediocre levels of desire and love. Fidelity is no effort. If it were, there'd be no merit to it. Wanting to go to bed with someone and not doing so out of respect for your partner, would in fact be the greatest proof of a lack of respect for him or her.

Nonetheless, despite the good intentions, her girlish face, the cream on her nose, the eggs in the eggcups and palms on shop-windows, after three months of living together they have their first domestic. It's very hard to pin down exactly why. After squabbling long and hard, they don't remember clearly how they got like that or who started it. She goes off to their bedroom to write about it in her diary: a children's edition illustrated with drawings of Pluto the dog he gave her as a joke-present. Tears stream down her cheeks and splash on the page. She scrawls that from now on nothing will ever be the same between them. The blindfold has fallen from her eyes, and it's given her a fright. When she says 'enough,' it means 'enough,' when she's with him she feels *paradoxically* at her loneliest, and she'd like to know which of the two is the real Ernest: the one she knew or the one who took his mask off today.

After half an hour he knocks at the door.

'Go away, please, I don't want you to see me like this,' she whimpers. And she's sorry he obeys because she is very pretty when she cries.

The scene of unrequited forgiveness is repeated twice. For his third attempt, Ernest slips a sheet of paper under the door on which he describes himself as an idiot. She tries to read it without getting out of bed, but her eyesight isn't that good. And it would be wrong to go and get it. That would be showing too much interest, it would seem like she's over it already. But she's bored. She's written down all she had to write. She'd grab a book, but that's wrong too, it would mean she's no longer sad and can enjoy reading. In the end she decides to get up, read the sheet on the ground as quickly as she can, and go back to bed as if she's not taken a look.

He's lying on the sofa and doesn't know what to do. He can't switch the television on, because she'd never forgive him. It's inappropriate. He can't grab a sandwich either, that would also be wrong. A shot of whisky would be right. Generally speaking, drinking high-proof spirits is always all right. On the other hand, swigging weak alcohol, like beer, hardly comes in that category. Beer-drinking is too party-like.

But if he doesn't eat, the whisky will go to his head. He could pour himself a whisky and have a bite to eat, but what? Crisps are totally out of the question. A banana or slice of cheese might be all right, but, in any case, he now realises, it would be quite wrong for her to hear him open the fridge. And reading the newspaper – she'd also hear the rustle of the pages turning – would be the most inappropriate act ever, he gets bored and finally drags himself back to their bedroom. He knocks, and, as he gets no reply, half-opens the door and sticks his nose in.

'Please forgive me?' he asks mournfully. 'I'm a shit.'

She screws her face up like a little kid. She tries to ensure he sees her tears have made the ink run in her notebook. She's shattered, but after giving it a moment's thought, she thinks it highly praiseworthy that he's come to apologise – it shows his personality – so she screws her face up even more and, in a clownish voice, whimpers: 'Ye-essh…' She means 'yes,' evidently. He just has to smile. He also curls his lower lip, like a clown, pretending to be sad: 'D'yer shtill lerve meee?'

'Mmm…' she responds doubtfully in the same tone. 'Dunno, shy dunno. And youhoo?'

'Veree merch!'

She opens her arms out like an actress in a children's theatre. He throws himself gratefully into them. She cuddles him, because it's what she always says: humour comes top in her scale of values. It is absolutely vital – and she can never emphasise this enough – to be able to laugh at oneself. And she thinks that in this sense, Ernest is changing. He's gradually freeing up the child he carries within. He's letting himself go.

The day after their mutual respect grows in leaps and bounds. She decides to go to bed to read before him: she gives him a kiss and takes her book. How nice not to be angry and to be able to read. He says, if she doesn't mind, he'll stay and surf the internet awhile. How nice not be angry and to be able to surf. She puts on her pyjamas with the puppets tumbling out of a box. It's hot, but she's got to keep up her image: little girls or female clowns don't sleep naked. Once she's in bed she remembers: she should have drunk some water. She moves as if to get up but then changes her mind. He'll think it funny if she calls out. 'Daddy! Shime shirsty!' she screeches, adopting yesterday's cute little voice. She keeps it up until he hears her and says he's coming, laughing himself silly.

'Issh my little cutchicoo shirsty? Shou shirsty, my big babby?' He runs off to get the water, and comes back behaving like a servant.

She takes the glass in both hands, like a two-year old. When she's drunk it, she opens her eyes wide and sighs with pleasure: 'Agh!' she pretends to burp. He continues the joke and pats her on the back.

Over the next two months they go on squabbling and speaking like this whenever they make peace. But also when one asks the other for something. They soon extend their hours and on Sunday morning, after reading the Sunday supplements, she usually says: 'Daddy... shtime for drinky-dinks?'

Though one can't pick out a starting-date, or any act that set it off, well into the fourth month of their relationship they are both speaking baby-talk most of the time, unless they have something important or hopefully original to tell each other. Only in such cases, to give proper emphasis, do they adopt their normal tone of voice. They use their normal voices when they come out of the cinema and loudly debate the film: 'A really clichéd ending,' he ventures.

'Could have done without the last twenty minutes,' she replies.

They also speak normally when they criticise the presenter of the programme for which she does scripts and comedy, because he is predictable, uncultured, a poseur and doesn't get intelligent humour. But they talk baby-talk for everyday chitchat ('What shall we do for dinner?' 'Shall we go for a drink?' 'I can't stand your father'). They get so into the habit it sometimes slips out in public. When they're alone they whimper in delight: 'Incredible, we can't keep it under control when we're in company.'

They wonder if other people would understand them if they heard them speak like that. They conclude they wouldn't.

'It would be the end of my career,' she exclaims.

'Just imagine if it slipped out on mike?' he speculates.

'Whatsh shwerd happern to ussh?'

'Shi dunno!'

In their fifth month, they baby-talk messages to each other on the answering machine. In the sixth, she uses it to talk to her mother on the phone. In the seventh, so does he.

Sex lost its novelty some time ago. They can no longer paw each other on the sofa, crumpling the throw and clattering the remote on the floor in a moment of passion. It would go on too long and make them dependent on the television or think about their own things. If he gives her a few smacking kisses in an advert break, she lets him, but as soon as she can, she runs off to the bedroom imitating the tottering gait of a little girl in nappies. He follows behind with his trousers round his ankles, like a penguin. It's inevitable then, that another day – now into the eighth month or so – when they're in bed he asks her: 'Shome shheerr, my lervvly. Shyou-oo itchy-itchy for a mouthy-mouthy?'

And she replies trying to sound enthusiastic: 'Shick shyour shaushage in shyoor babby...'

About to orgasm, he moans: 'Don't shtop, don't shtop, mee-mee shcummiiin...'

And she shouts: 'Yessh, yessh, yeeeshh...!'

After this episode they talk the baby-talk all the time: it's not amorous anymore and is just a habit. Now when they leave the cinema, he says: 'Shuuper clishéd, washn't it?'

And she responds bored out of her mind: 'Shcould dun shwithoutsh lash shwenty minush.'

In the middle of month nine they have the biggest row in their life as a couple. It's difficult to pin down why exactly. After arguing for so long they can't even remember why they got into that state or who started it. He spends the night on the sofa and she goes to work without speaking to him. When she gets back, she closes the bedroom door and disconsolately starts writing in her diary how itsh dishicult to do shradio shumor in momentsh like theshe. In the evening he knocks on the door and says very seriously: 'I begsh you to foorgive mee.'

She shouts: 'Don shyoou dare toush me, shyooou shlittel shwine!' And bursts into tears.

She seems really sad over the next month. She stops painting smiles on their eggs, smearing cream over her nose and steaming up shop-windows. When he screws his face up like a clown in the TV breaks and asks her if she wantsh a shuge saushage, she responds: 'I don't fancy a man who talks like an idiot. If you want to fuck, don't treat me like a little kid.'

The day they've known each other for a year, they row in the supermarket over the price of the bottle of wine they're going to take to a party at the presenter's place. As a result they arrive late.

'Itss the lash shime shi do shat,' he promises her in the lift.

'Speak properly, man. You make me feel hysterical,' she complains. 'If you treat me like a minor again, I'll leave.'

They make peace a second before the presenter opens the door. His skin's ultra-violet ray black, he's wearing a skin-tight T-shirt and riding boots with a small heel. He's very drunk. Inside, everyone's dancing.

'Come in and leave your coats on the bed,' he suggests in that husky voice that has made him a star on radio. 'I'm up to fuckin' here with work.'

This strikes her as the expression of a man of the world. Of a mature adult. Suddenly he doesn't seem predictable or a poseur. Maybe she felt he was predictable and a poseur under her boyfriend's influence.

For the next half an hour Ernest tries to dance uninhibitedly to please her. He keeps up his witty patter. But she shakes him off and loses him entirely by going on to the terrace. The presenter's there and offers her a drink. They sit on the wicker chairs, and she tucks her knees under her chin. It's so strange, she thinks, we're fed up with the sight of one another at the radio but here it's as if we've never met. We've never really had what you'd call a decent chat. It's true.

Two minutes later, he starts telling her he has an idea in his head for a television programme. She immediately looks interested. (She likes talking to someone more adult.) The programme will be magazine-style with people talking (it won't be the traditional telly discussion, but women in debate), a mobile camera unit (who won't go the usual places, but to odd ones) and a de-dramatising epilogue, where an actor will tell stories from everyday life that we've all experienced (like say 'all there is in the fridge is a yoghurt past its sell-by date'). He wants to present the idea to a producer, but, as he makes so many spelling-mistakes (so many his Word spellchecker doesn't recognise the language), he can't think who to give it to get clean copy. Àngels offers to clean it up for him. Happy to find someone to clean up his text, the presenter says it's really great being with her on the terrace and that Ernest is very lucky. Àngels smiles (it's a sad smile) and pats her skirt a couple of times so the cat jumps up. Nobody can know how frustrating it is to live with someone as infantile as Ernest. The presenter puts his feet on the balustrade and starts rolling a joint: 'It's a real pleasure talking to you, Àngels. Talking to women is different to talking to men. You are more intelligent.'

'I find it a real pleasure talking to you. I'm glad you're so mature and so unpredictable. I can't stand predictable men.'

When they embrace, the cat miaows in irritation and leaps on to the ground. After that kiss she opens her eyes intensely and smiles. She puts one hand over her mouth and waves the other, as if she were a naughty child who's misbehaved.

'Do you know you've got a very naïve little face?' he compliments her. And he looks at her through a square formed by the thumbs and index fingers of both hands, as if he were a film-director. 'You're like a little girl. You're a little clown. You've got a little girlsh fashe, nobody ever told you?'

And she opens her eyes even wider, screws her face up like a little kid and makes him laugh.

Learn to Wine-Taste

'Here you are,' says Mrs Salmeron. And she hands Mrs Biosca a nine-euro bottle of wine. 'Put it in the fridge.'

Mrs Biosca examines the label and the half-torn off price: 'Oh! I'd rather thought you'd bring a wine from the course.'

The Salmerons and the Bioscas met on a wine-tasting course. From the very first day Mrs Salmeron tried to sit next to Mrs Biosca and Mrs Biosca finally invited them to dinner. The Salmerons have come dressed up to the nines. The Bioscas, on the other hand, greet them in casual around-the-house clothes: she is wearing a kind of white tracksuit, and he is in shabby jeans and a T-shirt with the image of one black sheep in a flock of white.

'Maria!' shouts Mrs Biosca. The smallest door of all opens and in walks a maid. The Salmerons give her their bag and coats.

'Come in,' says Mrs Biosca.

They follow her almost swooning with pleasure. They'd imagined the Bioscas were rich but never that they'd have a maid or such a luxurious flat. Indeed, the husband is always unshaven and uses a big old-fashioned mobile. Everywhere there are old, padlocked trunks, next to standard lamps, and white sofas and armchairs in front of the trunks and lights.

A little boy in a baby-gro is playing on the carpet in the dining room.

'Àlvar, what are you doing here?' his mother asks when she sees him. She lifts him up by the armpits. 'Poo-poos?'

'Look how they know…' says Mrs Salmeron

apprehensively, for the sake of saying something.

Mrs Biosca puts the nappy level with her nose and sniffs.

'Yes, you've got poos. Oh and in quantity...' And she clicks her tongue in disgust.

'More shit already?' her husband asks incredulously. 'I've only just changed him!'

She hands the child on and the man also grabs him by the armpits, shakes him, puts the nappy level with his nose and sniffs. (Mr Salmeron thinks about their wine tasting course.) It's confirmed: the kid's filled his nappy.

'Change him for me, *amore*,' wife asks husband. 'I'm seeing to the dinner.'

Mrs Salmeron is surprised the maid doesn't look after the kid, but says nothing. She follows Mrs Biosca into the kitchen. She knows that she is into nouvelle cuisine, she's always talking about it and she imagines they'll dine on one delicacy after another. She's lectured her man on his duty to swallow whatever's put before him without pulling a face and particularly to keep quiet if he's left feeling hungry. But she now sees that the food couldn't be simpler. There's cold soup, she thinks, and lamb cutlets in bread crumbs.

'Can I help?' she says. 'What can I do? You tell me.'

'Such hyperactivity,' complains Mrs Biosca with a smile. 'Off to the dining room, go on, the Philly will help me.'

There's a dog in the laundry-room off the kitchen. Its owner lets it out, and the noise of its nails scraping over the parquet makes Mrs Salmeron's teeth grate anxiously. It's big and black and its ears and tail have been clipped. Its starts barking furiously opposite her, and Mrs Biosca shuts it back in. The howls of protest go on and on.

'He didn't like you,' says Mrs Biosca jokingly. But Mrs Salmeron feels offended. She goes back to the dining room where Mr Salmeron is lolling on the sofa looking at the ceiling. Mr Biosca has gone off to change the kid.

'He let me in on a few things,' he whispers.

'What?'

'They're going to a Psychiatrists' Congress in three days, half as a holiday, and leaving the boy with his mother, but…'

'Don't they have their nanny?'

Mr Salmeron twitches as if he'd felt a pain in his neck. He's annoyed his wife takes on the language and ways of the Bioscas so easily. You bet that one day on the course she heard the other woman talking about her 'nanny' and now she's also using that word to be like her. Why couldn't she use a good old Catalan word like 'mainadera', rather than say 'nanny'? Why must she impoverish the language?

'And it seems they've nobody to take the dog for a walk.' He goes on. 'I think they'll ask us.'

Mr Biosca's back: 'Don't ever have children, believe me.'

He's just passing the time of day, but Mrs Salmeron thinks it's a good topic for conversation and engages enthusiastically.

'We've thought about it. But it would mean one of us giving up work, or else…'

Mr Salmeron is getting more and more nervous. It's gone half past ten and they should have started dinner some time ago. He's a nice, affable fellow, but if he doesn't eat on time, he gets surly and aggressive. To keep hunger at bay, he digs into the crisps in a dark wooden bowl that's on top of a book: *The Alchemist of the Stove*.

'We buy them in a very small delicatessen. They make them themselves. By hand,' Mr Biosca announces.

'By hand?' asks Mrs Salmeron as enthusiastically as ever. She tastes a hand-made crisp even more enthusiastically and says you can tell it's hand-made, you really can. You can easily tell it's hand-made, and by a long chalk. She'd just been talking about our grandparents' healthy eating habits and the fact her Gabriel (Mr Salmeron) doesn't like green vegetables, but when he eats an artichoke, the real article, as in the good old days, those cooked by his grandma naturally, he really can tell. Or tomatoes, he doesn't like them either, but he really knows when it's the real thing.

'Oh, well, I think we've got tomato for dinner,' says Mr Biosca, not at all apologetically. 'We're on a diet.'

Mrs Biosca comes out of the kitchen and rubs her hands as if everything is ready. Rather than sit down, she perches her bum on the arm of a sofa.

'Shall we have dinner? Are you hungry?' asks Mr Biosca. Mr Salmeron stands up.

'Did he go to sleep?' asks Mrs Biosca.

Her husband shrugs his shoulders and Mrs Salmeron immediately offers to go and check. The parents protest frightened she might wake him up, but to no purpose. She disappears down a passage. They hear her opening the wrong doors laughing like a mad woman each time she gets it wrong until she gets it right. They know she's got it right because they then hear her speaking to the boy in a baby talk. She returns two minutes later, all dishevelled and with a stain on her leather jacket. 'He brought his food back up, but don't worry,' she says smiling nervously. 'His eyes are wide open.'

'You'd better clean it now or it will never go,' his mother warns.

Mr Salmeron looks at the patch apprehensively. It smells of kefir. But his wife, who'd have gone on and on in a restaurant till they brought a stain remover, refuses to use water. No way. Mr Biosca takes this opportunity to go and look at the kid.

'Shall we sit down?' suggests Mrs Biosca.

But the three of them stand to attention in front of the table; a handsome wood table – Mrs Salmeron recognises this immediately – of the kind you might inherit. Theirs, on the other hand, is glass with a green marble leg in the shape of a sail. Once Mr Biosca is back, she asks: 'Where do you sit normally? Don't do things differently for our sake, please.'

They spread themselves around, and the maid appears on cue with the soup tureen. She stands next to Mrs Salmeron who is slow to realise it's self-service. Then it's their hostess's turn and then Mr Salmeron's. His wife is suffering in case he says he doesn't want any, but she sees him fill his bowl and start slurping.

'Gabi!' she nags him with that irritated smile she adopts in company. As he apparently doesn't understand why she's nagging, she's obliged to add: 'It is delicious, but perhaps you could wait?'

Mr Salmeron gives her a withering look when he hears her say 'delicious'. She never uses the word 'delicious'.

'No, don't worry. Let him start!' Mrs Biosca interjects magnanimously. Mrs Salmeron, on the other hand, provokes a ripple of sympathy towards her husband.

'He's like a big baby...!' she shouts trying to excuse him.

'Thank you, Maria,' says Mrs Biosca.

But the maid can't possibly be a Maria, Mrs Salmeron ruminates. Or could she? Perhaps she's given her that name to help her along in life or maybe she's not Vietnamese, as she imagined, and is from the Philippines. 'Philly', it then strikes her, must be short for 'Philippine'.

'Delicious!' she repeats enthusiastically. 'What is it? What is it? Tomato soup?'

'Gazpacho,' the other responds, 'but we make a light version. We don't use pepper or bread, and practically no vinegar. We're dieting.'

Once Mrs Salmeron has finished praising their gazpacho, Mrs Biosca resumes her chattering: 'As I was saying: we're going away and our nanny is on holiday. The boy will stay with my mother, but...'

'Who will look after your dog?' asks Mrs Salmeron.

'Ah! That's a taboo subject,' Mrs Biosca replies jokingly. And she makes a cross with her two little fingers, as if warding off the devil or a vampire.

'We ought to leave him in a holiday kennel or hire a dog-walker, but we don't like that idea,' adds Mr Biosca. 'The

Philly's on holiday and the nanny's going to Combray. She is from Combray. We've got a very Proustian nanny.' The Salmerons smile, heads bowed, not knowing what to say. 'I'm not at all keen on leaving the dog by himself, with other dogs, you know… Freud is very special.'

'If only they allowed dogs in our hotel…' complains his wife. 'But the ones who ravage rooms, steal bathrobes and leave without paying are not the dogs.'

'No, they're not the dogs,' agrees Mrs Salmeron, 'but their masters!'

'People think because animals don't speak our language, they don't get depressed or have feelings,' declares Mr Biosca. 'Last time Freud came back so tense. They get down in the dumps as well. But you know all about that. What can I tell you?'

Mrs Salmeron twists her head and looks down. He is a psychiatrist of repute. She's a psychologist. She likes a psychiatrist like Biosca rating her professionally.

'If you like, we'll come and take him out,' she suggests. 'We were just talking about that, weren't we, Gabi?' But he says nothing.

Their hosts protest: 'No, you mustn't even offer.'

'No, it's the least we can do. No bother at all.'

'That's not why we mentioned it. Now you'll think… and it's not so.'

As the Bioscas resist forcefully, Mrs Salmeron also insists forcefully. In fact, she's now saying she won't accept 'no' for an answer.

'Let's see: are we going away? No, we're not. And what do we do all day by ourselves in Barcelona? What do we do? The dermatologist warned me not to go near the beach. It's not as if my skin has used up all its solar capital, it's really deep in debt!' She bursts out laughing and claps her hands. The Bioscas smile.

They give and take throughout the second course and Mrs Salmeron gets so embroiled that she only notices her hubby hasn't touched the cutlets when the maid comes to clear the table. He likes cutlets. If he ate the first course, that was tomato, why did he decide not to eat something he likes like the cutlets? Why's he acting that way? Every time Mr Biosca opened a bottle, Mr Salmeron refused to taste, as they'd learned how to on the course. She watches him pick at the cheeses and quince, for dessert, but he leaves them on his plate as well. And after a lengthy interlude, while they're nibbling low-calorie chocolate truffles (bought from a shop in London where you have to order them months in advance), they agree to come and take the dog out every day. Though Mrs Biosca asks only one favour of them: for them to come and stay in the flat. It's the least they can offer them.

'Come and stay?' queries Mr Salmeron. 'But we only live two minutes away!'

'Two minutes isn't really true, is it, Gabi?' his wife protests. If she has to choose between sucking up to her husband or someone else, it's always to someone else.

'If not, I'll feel really guilty,' laments Mrs Biosca, acting like a little girl. 'Just imagine you're on holiday in an apartment-hotel.'

And she uses the time the coffee's brewing to tell Mrs Salmeron where they keep the bed linen, the number of the grocery store and how the ice-maker works.

'Naturally, I'll leave the fridge full. Whatever you order from the grocers, and I mean whatever, will go on our account. Whatever it may be, Montse, you know me.' She holds her arms out and drops them, as if this were a gesture that encapsulated her generosity. 'I want this to be your second honeymoon.'

The next step is to meet the dog. 'Look, Freud, this is Gabriel (let him lick you) and this is Montse (stroke him, never raise your voice, Freud, we're friends, she's not going to hurt me, easy with your hand, he soon senses any aggression).' And, after she lets it sniff between her thighs, on a knife-edge because she's got her period and Mrs Biosca might notice, Mr and Mrs Salmeron finally crouch down and offer it a tin of his food. He growls at first, but then settles down.

Mrs Biosca says: 'The people who criticise this breed are complete ignoramuses.'

She leaves the dog in the dining-room, gives instructions to the maid, opens the doors of their library, which is where they'll take coffee, and stands to one side, inscrutable and self-assured, to let them walk in first.

'I was surprised you had so few books in the dining-room,' comments Mrs Salmeron, smiling like a perceptive slave.

'Oh, come now!' sighs Mrs Biosca. 'Always keep one's novels out of sight.' And she yawns loudly. 'Would you like a grappa or…?'

Mr Salmeron says he would and this makes Biosca hubby look at his watch. He shuts his eyes and acts as if he's half nodding off, quite brazenly. Mrs Salmeron hurries her husband: 'Come on, Gabi, they're tired…'

'No, not at all, finish your drink. Take your time,' the other's wife concedes. But they're already getting up.

The night after Mrs Biosca rings to say she's taking the dog for a walk and perhaps Mr Salmeron would like to accompany her to see how it's done. They both get dressed – they were already in their pyjamas – and take a taxi, because Mr Salmeron has the car in a good parking space. Mrs Biosca demonstrates how to collect up the turds in a bag. They must be sure to collect them up. Their neighbourhood isn't like some others, and Freud doesn't like the doggie-poo areas, he's very much his own dog. She recommends they bring boiled ham to win him over.

'But not the tinned sort that they make from potato and powdered bones,' she adds laughing nervously. And as they nod, also very nervously, she apologises: 'I know it's immoral, with the poverty there is in the world, to buy my dog best ham or Canary Island ham at thirty euros a kilo, but if I don't it's hardly going to help the starving. The other day the bank sent me a statement that said: "If you pay with your card, you've planted ten trees." At least I plant trees.'

The day after the Bioscas go to their Congress, the Salmerons are still at home when the wife calls them on her mobile from the airport: 'Freud told me his tummy is rumbling like mad.'

'We're just off,' Mrs Salmeron apologises.

'Hey, I was only joking. I'm phoning to tell you something you'll find very amusing.' And she tells them that the dog cried a lot, because when he saw the suitcases he understood he was going to be left by himself. Canine intuition is really incredible.

The Salmerons have a row on the way over because of the ham. She insisted on going to buy it in the delicatessen in the area where the Bioscas live, and not in the supermarket where they always go. They'll spend almost three hundred euros in the two weeks if they're going to give it best ham every day, but Mrs Salmeron won't hear of charging it to them. On the other hand, he says he doesn't intend giving them it as a present. As the Bioscas don't think twice about three hundred euros, they'd not thought to tell the Salmerons they'd pay when they get back.

Excited and nervous she confronts the porter. Her husband brings up the rear dragging their suitcase, mincing along like a man who feels affronted.

'Good afternoon,' his wife begins.

And then explains they are friends of the Bioscas. They're temporarily moving into their flat in order to walk their dog. The porter looks up from his newspaper and ask her for her ID number, but doesn't believe her when she recites it: he demands to see her card. He's never done this before, but she *is* acting very strangely. Mr Salmeron walks on the red carpet as if he were squeezing water from his trouser legs. He doesn't dare open the lift-door, in case the porter refuses them entry. They walk in and press the button to the 4th. Mrs Salmeron looks at herself in the mirror. She's dressed up as if she were going to her psychologists' consultancy to work; a lacy blouse and jeans tucked inside her high boots. She's also wearing a pearl necklace with an imitation gold clasp. She doesn't want to feel out of place in the neighbourhood.

'I really feel like a beer,' he whinges, like a spoilt brat.

On their way over she'd been telling him he could help himself to whatever he fancies, but suddenly takes fright: 'Don't start asking for things like that. You've got as much beer as you can hold at home, and you never look at the stuff. Don't let's take advantage, right? If they've left champagne, you'll drink champagne. Whether you like it or not.'

He takes the keys out of his pocket and selects the flat one from the bunch, which is to the Bioscas' security door.

'You got the number?' she asks in that pleasant tone she uses when she feels irremediably stressed.

He says he has very rudely. He takes the paper with the number to disconnect the alarm out of the same pocket: number 4509. Bet it's the same for the credit card and the safe. Four thousand five hundred and nine. The Salmerons have one number for everything but it's not as big.

'Try to stop it ringing, will you?'

Once he's disconnected it successfully she loves him again. She rewards him with a kiss. But if he'd made a mistake, she'd have lost her cool, would have started to cry and perhaps even hit him. She's not like this normally. Only when she's doing things for others.

'Come on, Gabi,' she starts to organise him. 'First of all, down to work: you take the beast for a walk and in the meantime I'll do a bit of dusting and set the table. When you get back, we'll eat whatever they've left us.'

He shakes his head as if dealing with a lunatic.

'A bit of dusting? Why do you have to dust? Are you a maid? Are they paying you to do that?'

He puts the key in the lock and they hear barking. She unwraps the packet of ham as quickly as she can. He touches the wall looking for the switch and puts the light on. He pushes the suitcase inside.

The dog is shut in the sitting room, but is attacking the glass door leading to the lobby as if it's strong enough to break it. The Salmerons realise straight away that things aren't going to plan.

'Freud, darl…'

'We're Montse and Gabi, friends of Mariola. Where's Mariola?'

It barks even louder when it hears her name, but maybe that's a coincidence.

'We've brought the ham you like.'

If they try to approach the door to throw its food in, it goes crazy and, when they retreat, it growls between its teeth, so they sit down in the chairs in the lobby and wait for it to calm down. If only they could go into the kitchen or the toilet. But from where they are they only have access to the sitting room. The steps lead to the maid's room that is locked. Minutes tick by. They feel incredibly on edge because the snarling doesn't abate. It's impossible not to think about the noise. Impossible not to think that the neighbours – if they're in – won't complain, and that the porter won't come. Mrs Salmeron is already crying, and her husband, twitching, turns the glass-door handle and tries to open it a crack, but the animal hurls itself at the glass yet again – now not barking but howling – and retreats in a state of shock.

He drags over one of the armchairs to prop against the door. They argue. Mr Salmeron says that if the dog hasn't shut up in half an hour, they should go home – he, at least, intends to go home. His wife thinks it's unlikely it will quieten down in half an hour, but she agrees. And sees how the minutes pass and it doesn't let up. It must think the Salmerons are thieves. They must have taught it always to bark whenever anyone enters the flat. And it must think the Salmerons – the people who have to walk it, feed it and pick up its turds – are responsible for the absence of the Bioscas. Where must the

Bioscas be now? In a hotel with other psychiatrists, wine-tasting and chatting about this and that. But who knows what the beast is thinking? Perhaps it's got the idea in its little doggie-brain that they've killed its owners. Mrs Salmeron can't stop crying. She's crying more than when her father died.

'We'll have to ring a vet and get him to give it a tranquilliser,' she moans. 'It's never going to stop. It won't let us go in.'

They start arguing again because he wants to ring the Bioscas, and she shouts they can't, he can't because if he calls them she'll never forgive him. She doesn't want the Bioscas to have to abandon their congress and rush back here because they can't handle their dog.

It's getting dark. Mrs Salmeron repeats they have to dare go in, open the door for a minute and throw in some food, but he doesn't want to, because he thinks the dog might easily bite his hand off. And he repeats that he wants to go home. But they don't budge, because they're both imagining the desolate panorama inside, the furniture upside down and the piles of shit. If they don't feed it now, it will be even hungrier and wilder tomorrow and things will get worse. And when they've been waiting for an hour, and still not come to a decision, because the dog hasn't stopped barking for a single moment, they start eating the ham.

The Importance of Oral and Dental Hygiene

What he most craves in the world is to live with her. Why can't they share that flat her parents let her use for a nominal rent? And who says flat has to mean breakfast, nights in watching the telly, and the message on the answering machine. He wants her to fall ill just so he can look after her. If half of the couple has to be prostrate in a coma, let it be her. Because he will always love her, even if she is prostrate in a coma. If only he could show her. On the other hand, should the reverse happen, and he's the one prostrate in a coma, please, please unplug him. He couldn't let her make such a sacrifice, not for anything in the world.

All in all, he's blissfully happy when, one night, she and her suitcases turn up on his doorstep. The only cloudlet darkening his horizon of joy is the thought that if she's prostrate in a coma, the person who most loves her in the world (himself) won't have the right to care for her. They won't have co-habited long enough. Just a few hours. Her carer would be Juande, her ex-boyfriend, who lived with her six months to some purpose. And in hospital, everybody would tearfully hug Juande. It would make him really jealous. He'd do anything for time to rush by so he could show the world that it's him (and not Juande) who really loves her and it should be him caring for her if she's prostrate in a coma. He's desperate to set up routines with her. To say 'we like doing this and that.' We. The word 'we' gives him the shakes. He hugs her, kisses her eyelids and promises to make her ever so happy.

While she's hanging her clothes up in the wardrobe, he goes down to the 24-hour chemists to buy two toothbrushes. One yellow; one red. Symbols of their love. He rushes upstairs to wave them at her.

'Which colour do you like best?'

'I don't mind,' she replies. 'You choose.'

How disappointing. He was hoping she'd throw herself into his arms, cover *his* eyelids in kisses and say: 'Two toothbrushes in one glass in the bathroom! They're symbolically starting out their new lives together with us.' But, seemingly, she doesn't think the small things are important. She couldn't care less about the small things. And she doesn't and never did possess the gift of symbolic thought. She just sees two toothbrushes, not the token of a pledge.

'OK, I'll have the yellow one, OK?' he asks despondently.

'Yes,' she replies. 'I don't care what colour I have.'

Head bowed, he enters the bathroom and cleans his teeth with his new brush. When he's finished, he rinses his mouth, puts the bristles under the spurting water and runs his thumb over them. He puts his in the glass next to hers. As he can see she'll be a while sorting her clothes out, he decides to start cooking two plain omelettes and smearing tomato over the bread. If she'd given him some notice, he'd have bought candles and champagne. (She only says she loves him if she's drunk.) But maybe it's nicer this way. They're the first plain omelettes and tomato bread in their new life. They've eaten lots of omelettes in this flat, but never as a couple, and he tries to savour the situation to the full. He's cooking two omelettes: one, medium, for himself, and one rarer, for the lady in his life. When he's set the table, he shouts: 'Dinner's ready!'

He goes all goose-pimply. From now on, he'll repeat this everyday phrase ('Dinner's ready') every night and after many such nights will no longer experience the thrill he feels now when uttering those words. Even if, quite frankly, it upsets him to think he's not the first to say them to her. Juande, her ex, must also have summoned her to the dinner table. And you bet he didn't appreciate it when he did. It'll be months before he's shouted 'Dinner's ready' as often as Juande.

When they've sat down, they drink to their new life with wine that was left over in the fridge, but he's on such a high he's already looking forward to the moment when they collect up the dishes and wash up together. She's never done that before because when she came to dinner she was always 'his guest'. From now on, after their omelettes, they'll toil together in the kitchen in their own aprons. He mustn't forget to buy her one. The jokey sort. With a recipe, or embossed breasts. Or one like his. Which says: 'Chef's secret trick: dine out.'

That's why he's so down in the dumps, when she's scoured her yoghurt pot and announces she's got her period and would rather leave sorting the kitchen to the morning.

'But it'll only take a moment,' he tries to argue. 'The two of us can do it in a jiffy.'

She stretches out on the sofa and places both hands over her left ovary: 'Now we're together we ought to buy a dishwasher, don't you think?'

The idea she wants a dishwasher deflates him. It means she doesn't get as much fun as he does from washing up together, gossiping and splashing one another. He re-visits the bathroom and brushes his teeth again. When he comes out, she's waiting in the passage, Tampax in hand.

'You finished in there?'

He says he has, quite taken aback. If she wanted to go to the toilet, why didn't she go in when he was in there? He understands nothing. They're a couple now. And couples meet up in the bathroom. Everybody knows the toilet is the place where you remind one another of what needs buying or exchange views on a film. One sits on the bowl while the other layers the cream on or casually tidies their hair in front of the mirror.

He goes back to tidy the kitchen and hears her put the door on the catch. The click from that catch shatters his heart. What *is* this secret thing she can't share with him? Maybe it's a poo? In that case, is she afraid that if he goes in and smells the smell, he'll not idealise her any more? She clearly doesn't understand his love for her. It can't be her period. He wants to know all about her period: how many days it lasts, the brand and size of her tampons (whether they're mini, normal or super). He wants to buy them for her. He wants to see her putting it in. He wants to put it in, wants to take it out.

He hears the catch again and the door open. She's humming a jingle from an advert. She walks into the kitchen and throws a ball of toilet paper wrapped round her dirty Tampax into the bin. She asks: 'Hey, wasn't my toothbrush the red one?'

'Yes,' he replies. 'Why?'

'Because someone's used it. You used both of them.'

He looks at her, his tears welling. So what if he got the wrong toothbrush and used hers?

'Don't worry, you won't catch Aids…' he mutters, in a huff.

'I know, silly. It was only an idle comment.'

But the idle comment really hurt. Perhaps she finds a toothbrush that's had contact with his mouth repulsive? If she finds the toothbrush that's had contact with his mouth repulsive, what else might repel her? Tongue-kissing him, perhaps? Putting his penis in her mouth? What does she really feel when she swallows his semen? If she loves him as much as *he* loves her, she wouldn't get upset because he'd used her toothbrush. Quite the contrary. She'd love the idea that their salivas were mixing. It's the first day of their life together and she's already putting down markers. She said she wants a dishwasher, she put the toilet door on the catch, and now, to cap it all, she's nagging him because he used the wrong toothbrush. What will she do next?

The Benefits of Maternal Lactancy

'Hector, do you mind holding the cloud straight, so I can staple it?' Laura Garriga asks her lad. But he just clings to the cardboard and stares at the ground. 'Come on, put a bit of energy into it.'

Garriga can understand why: it's boring for an adolescent to spend Sunday morning with his mother, and he wouldn't be there if she'd had a say in it. He'd have stayed at home as he wanted, doing his own thing. Enjoying his personal time, as the psychologist says. But Garriga's ex doesn't think it's right for him to spend so many hours by himself in front of the computer screen, while she devotes herself to the Association. Her ex is always making fun of the Association.

They got to the park at eight o'clock. The event starts at ten, but all the Association members first have to blow up the balloons with the helium-pump they've rented, hang the banner on the stage and put the plastic chairs in a circle, so the women can all sit and suckle together. They are celebrating International Maternal Lactancy Day, but, besides that, this year, which is the fifth, they want to set a new Guinness World Record for women giving milk in unison.

'Do you know I've been non-stop at the media to interview me as chairwoman?' she tells him.

'*The media*?' he retorts scornfully.

'Hector, I'm trying to have a conversation with you. What do you want me to say then? Radio and telly? Right then radio and telly. I went to a radio station yesterday.'

'Which programme?'

'One that's called "Women's Things".' She's surprised he's interested. 'You heard of it?'

'No, I thought you'd probably gone to "Up Yours".'

He half laughs, and Garriga, when she hears that, gets all nervy. She starts asking him about the times and content of 'Up Yours'.

'Please, Mum, don't try to act all young and with it. It doesn't suit you. It's an 'extreme' programme. Satisfied? And don't get all hysterical and start shouting about it, because it's illegal and I don't want it to be closed down.'

She runs her tongue across her gums. She can't think what kind of 'extreme' he's referring to, whether 'extreme right' or 'extreme left'. She and her ex inculcated him with the values of the left, and 'Up Yours' seems more like a left-wing name. But maybe it *is* extreme left. Would the extreme left be preferable to the extreme right? And would the extreme left be preferable to the right full stop? Obviously he probably only listens in for the music and doesn't share its radical ideas. She breast-fed her son to the age of two. People are more intelligent and sensitive if they're breast-fed. That's been proven. And build up more defences. Her Hector, as a baby, had the usual four illnesses, though nothing serious. She believes – and is proud to say that hindsight has proved her right – that taking your children off the tit at a male doctor's say-so is just one more macho ploy.

'As you're so strong, why don't you help me put the fences up behind the stage?' she suggests.

His female psychologist reckons that, at this age when he's in a process of change and discovering his own body, it can't be bad (or sexist) to praise his physical strength. She's been taking him to the psychologist for the last two months, ever since school told them he seemed apathetic. He could do more than he does, because he finds it easy, but doesn't want to. So they say.

'Give me some money,' he demands. 'I've been holding

this little cloud up for hours.'

'If you don't speak properly I can't understand you. And if I can't understand you, I can't give you an answer and we can't speak, Hec…'

'Give-me some mo-ney…'

'Sorry, Hector, if your mother appears so *one-track minded*, but have you spent your pocket money?'

He wearily scratches a scab on his wrist. He lets go of the cloud, pokes around her bag and poles until he finds her purse. Garriga tries to look the other way while he does this. There are almost twenty mothers in the park. The Association's treasurer, who's expecting twins, is drawing coloured nipples on the balloons they're draping on the oleanders, and the secretary puts African music on the sound system (she's shacked up with an Ethiopian). It's a pity, thinks Garriga, a beggar has sat down on one of the benches – complete with transistor, cardboard boxes and metal supermarket trolley – because he's a blot on their show. The Palomares, Mariners and Mari Bustillo, an under-age single mother, have arrived.

'Mari, I'm so pleased you've come and it heartens me you're so keen to participate,' she gushes. And immediately says hello to the baby girl in the pushchair: 'And who's this little cutie-pie? Is it Sheila? It's little cutchi-coo, pretty cutchi-coo Sheila! And isn't your mother boootiful! A boootiful mum who'll behave herself today and not do any stirring, right? What'ch a luvly little thing, is che isn't che? Why'chu come? Hey? Hey? Why'chu come with that cute lickle pushy-chair?' She mentions that because the Association got her the (three-wheeled and all-weather) pushy-chair.

Bofill and Cáceres have come as well; two mothers who've adopted and come along in a spirit of solidarity, and Guimaraes: the latter hasn't got a pushy-chair, is carrying her baby round her neck, and is accompanied by her big son.

Garriga goes over discreetly to Adela. She's written the sketches.

'Trouble in store, Adela. Assuncão Guimaraes hasn't

come by herself.'

'It could be worse,' the other mutters, striking a deliberately tragic pose. 'She could have brought the whole *troop* along.' She's referring to her husband and the patriarch, who always come with her to meetings. The woman's in mourning from head to toe. In contrast, her big son is wearing check trousers that hang down below the top of his underpants.

'Great, Assuncão,' Garriga greets her, stroking the suckling baby. 'Great, really great to have you here.'

And adds she can understand that, because she's black and Brazilian and mightn't want to participate in this kind of act, and that's why she's so grateful she's come to offer her support. Or rather, they're all grateful, all the women are very grateful, not just her. She says hi to the adolescent: 'Hi, Sidónio. Your father and brothers gone to the fairground today?' But he doesn't reply. He scowls and walks off.

Garriga prays her son doesn't start talking to him. If God exists, 'Up Yours' must be far right and they won't be on speaking terms. Come to think of it, it's much better if he's on the far right. Only if God doesn't exist will he be on the far left and they'll be close buddies in five minutes.

She climbs on the platform and tests whether the microphone is working. She'd have liked her Hector to take an interest in the sound system. Sidónio Guimaraes is the one who doesn't miss a trick. But he doesn't miss a trick in a way that makes her suspicious.

'Hello, all you gals and guys. Welcome, sisters and brothers!' she starts off. She makes an effort to put females first, because the AGM voted that to say the male first was sexist as well. 'I hope I don't seem too much of a hopeless *commère*,' laughter all round. 'In a minute, I'll give you the game-plan for our celebration, OK? But, first of all, I wanted to say I hope this year the dads (and not just the usual suspects) really get stuck in!'

She reads out the list of the activities scheduled and

reminds everyone that, after the play, they'll be going for the Guinness Record.

'It was a secret, but you ought to know the telly people have confirmed they're coming to film us!'

Two Association members start giving out leaflets to the women in the circle and to passers-by. There are two beggars on the bench now, both reading very intently about the benefits of maternal lactancy. Garriga is looking for the adjudicator's number in her mobile contacts, in case he's got lost, when she sees her Hector coming over with the Guimaraes youth. God doesn't exist: from now on the Guimaraes youth will be round their place for dinner every night and want wine and fizzy pop. It'll be no good Garriga telling him it's not their style and that they believe in drinking water with their meals. The youth will only talk to her to ask for wine and fizzy pop and more bread (he dunks his bread into every course). In the end, he'll shut himself up with Hector in his bedroom and they'll look at porno sites on the internet. She gets down from the platform: 'Come here a minute, Hector, come here,' she shouts, so the Guimaraes youth realises she wants to speak privately to him. She wants to ask him, though not being racist in any way (because this isn't racist), if that youth is a good idea. But he doesn't budge.

'I wouldn't let him get away with that,' Adela chides her. And Garriga runs her tongue back over her gums. Adela's son is eight years old. And Hector, when he was eight, was as good as gold: nice and affectionate. He had playbooks where he drew her as a princess. (Even though they were always Republicans at home.) He went to a grant-aided, progressive-minded school. He took part in out-of-school activities. He's had all the freedom, dialogue and mother's milk he'd ever wanted.

'The separation's had a big impact on him,' she makes allowances for him. He comes out with all kinds of things. 'And I don't want to set him against his father or his new woman, I'm quite clear about that. I'm not going to do the castrating-witch bit.'

To cut that line of conversation short, she looks at her watch and beckons to one of the fathers. The man nods, climbs on stage and sits down at the electric piano. Everyone applauds, and some spectators click with their tongues as they learned to do at the hand-painting workshop (which they organised in order to integrate Moroccan women).

'Palomares is looking very tasty,' Garriga whispers half-heartedly.

'You must be joking. His bum's nothing to shout about,' Adela reproaches her, as if not appreciating Palomares's bum made her a person who knew nothing about men. They stare at him. He's wearing jeans and a T-shirt with a graphic of one black sheep amid a flock of white.

'Yes, his bum lets him down,' Garriga concedes, equally half-heartedly.

'Pernau's got the best bum. You take note from your women friends, who've been separated longer than you and know a thing or two about bums.'

The first scene begins. The character of a first-time mother goes to her doctor because her milk's not coming on tap and he's very macho and tells her not to worry because breast-feeding is not that important. When the audience hear him, they shout: 'Boo.' Then they perform the sketch about the sexist company that doesn't allow its workers to breastfeed, and the scene at the special cinema for lactating mothers. As the grand finale, the figure of the Pregnant Fairy appears in tight-fitting, sexy clothes. At the AGM they'd voted on whether such a character made the female body seem frivolous and the majority voted yes. Then they voted on whether, given the context, this was negative, and the vote indicated that it wasn't necessarily so. Depending on the situation, frivolity was a feminine value they should be reclaiming. All in all it could be very effective when it came to asserting the beauty of pregnant women. Frivolity was one thing, superficiality another. The sketches end on a lactancy rock number.

> Sisters, let's swing,
> rock it and fling!
> Ignore the posh medics,
> Stop popping their pills!
> Our babies champ at the bit,
> They want to get on the tit!

The two beggars clap to the music. Standing next to them Guimaraes has one breast naked and her baby's nuzzling there. When Garriga sees her she rushes over and grabs her arm in a fury. 'Bloody hell, Assuncão! Get into the circle, do it with us, can't you see that's what it's all about?'

But there's no way she's going to. She says nothing and laughs. Just shakes her head, no way, no way. And she doesn't stop laughing and her baby doesn't stop sucking. Adela goes over.

'But it's not the same doing it inside as outside.' She's trying to help. 'Don't you see we've come here today to show how we suckle our daughters and sons? Don't you think cultural difference should enrich, and not separate us?'

Garriga makes a gesture with her tense hands, as if to strangle her. On World Maternal Lactancy Day, all the women from the Progressive Milky Way Association sit in a circle breastfeeding, except for the one who's doing it three metres away.

'If we don't break the record because of you, I'll kill you!' she threatens through gritted teeth.

But her mobile rings: the people from the telly will get there late because they're filming squatters being chucked out and it's incredibly violent. While she's speaking, she has put a hand over her free ear so as not to hear the applause, the babies' crying and the final verse of the song:

If men were able to birth a baby
Breast-feeding would be… compulsory!

'Are you sure you don't want to sit inside the circle and do exactly the *same* as you're doing now?' she asks Guimaraes again once she's rung off. The other sways her head and laughs. She's now got her baby on her left nipple.

'If you don't join in, I'll have a word with Social Services!' she shouts.

'Racist!' retorts Guimaraes.

'That's all I need. Racist!' Garriga complains looking up to the heavens. 'So now I'm a racist precisely because I want to integrate her. Because I want it to be a big success and don't want her to be discriminated against, I'm a racist.'

She shakes her head in despair. What will the people from the telly think if they see all the mothers in the circle and the immigrant outside? They'll interview the one outside and ask her why she's not in there, or if somebody stopped her. She doesn't even want to imagine the news story: Guimaraes breastfeeding in one corner and two beggars getting their two cents in.

'Don't count on me next year. I'm not going to stand as chairwoman. I give up. I've had enough.'

But she changes her expression when she sees a man in a suit and tie with a leather briefcase appear, who has to be the adjudicator. She kisses him on both cheeks and asks him if he'd like anything.

'I could just do with a beer.'

Garriga gestures to Mari Bustillo to come over. She tells her slowly that the notary is thirsty and it would be an excellent idea if she went to buy him a beer from the bar. But Mari Bustillo refuses. She says she has to be in the park when the television people get there because she wants to make a statement in front of the cameras: her daughter's been coming from her Catalan nursery school the last three days with bog-standard nappies, when she took in a packet of extremely expensive, extra-drys, specially shaped for a baby's bottom. It's quite obvious someone is snaffling her extra-drys and she wants the case to be looked into, bottom by bottom, if necessary.

'The teachers must have made a mistake, Mari,' Garriga tries to calm her down. 'You've got to remember when little girls and boys *decide* to do a big poo, they all do it at the same time.'

And to convince her, she promises that if she fetches a beer for the adjudicator, she'll make a point of talking to the television people so they interview her. She gives her a ten-euro note and reminds her to get a receipt, whatever she does. And take her girl with her, for God's sake.

'I'm sorry,' Adela apologises. 'They've detected a personality disorder.'

'So I see,' mutters Garriga very solemnly. 'The less they've got up top, the more consumerist they become. It's the idiot box. The idiot box has colonised their brains.'

The man smiles and climbs up onto the platform with her. He sits down quite unembarrassed on the chair being used for the performance, puts his leather briefcase on his knees and opens it. He takes out a stopwatch and some forms.

'Can't we wait a wee while till the telly people get here?'

But he says that's impossible, for he's got to see to a record paella attempt immediately afterwards. Garriga sighs and picks up the microphone. She notices to her relief that the two beggars have gone. She gets so nervous she shouts: 'Hey, gals and guys, you all ready to unhook your bras when I get to three?'

The mothers say they are and so do the fathers, not thinking. She looks at her watch and starts the countdown. Deeply moved, she watches the twenty-nine women in the circle lift up their jerseys, remove their nipple pads and extract the dummies from their babies' mouths. Even the two mothers who've adopted give their babies bottles, blouses unbuttoned and breasts naked. The Guinness record attempt has officially begun. Some kids don't want to suckle, but Garriga reckons the adjudicator won't notice. In fact, he's looking at the spectacle as if he's under hypnosis. Now, a husband with long sideburns and a wisp of hair on his chin hisses that, if men gave birth, maternity leave would last three years.

'Mum!' her son then shouts. He's sat with Guimaraes on the bench where the two beggars were. Some of the women who hear him turn round to shut him up.

She gets down from the platform and walks over to him: 'Please, Hector,' she whispers. 'We're in the open air but try to preserve a little privacy.'

'Somebody's hiding over there and doing dirty things,' he informs her mischievously. And the Guimaraes youth tries to stop laughing. She's worried and peers at the clump of oleanders. Yes, someone is behind there, because the leaves are moving. But the fact her kid said it like that makes her fear the worst. She jumps over a palm that's acting as a barrier, her son and the Guimaraes youth in hot pursuit. They walk in single file across the flowerbed. She tries not to imagine it's Bustillo having a pee or forcing Sheila to drink beer. She's quite capable of that and much worse.

She sticks her head through the foliage and lets out a scream: the two beggars are there, their trousers round their ankles. The right hand of one is going up and down. Horrified, Garriga turns round to check if any of the women have seen it. They haven't.

'Get away, Hector!' She shouts between her teeth. 'Go away! Go away! Don't look!'

The two men are staring at the mothers massaging their breasts, taking them out, letting them flop, cradling them, putting them together, separating them, patting them, cleaning them and ensuring their kids are on nipple.

'Hey you,' she grunts, averting her gaze from their

sexual organs. 'Stop that or I'll call the police.'

One of them looks round at her, but carries on moving his hand up and down. Garriga steps back, frightened, in case he tries to attack her. Her son grabs a rock and threatens them. More intrepid, the Guimaraes youth starts kicking them in the ribs and manages to chase them to the most distant shrub. They don't forget their trolleys, but don't pull up their trousers. Garriga flops down on a chair and puts her hands over her face,

'Calm down, Mum…' her son consoles her. Adela and some Association members who heard the shouting have come over. The adjudicator, in contrast, is filling in the forms and hasn't blinked an eyelid.

'What did they do to you?' Adela asks Hector. 'Did they do something dirty to her?'

And she shakes her head; no, they didn't do anything. It was the two beggars, but they didn't mean to do anything. It's not their fault; they can't help being marginalised. She's over it and above all, they shouldn't say anything to their husbands, in case they get annoyed and want to call the event off. Tears fill her eyes.

'Next year you can get on with it. I've had enough. I want some time to myself,' she whimpers. And they all quickly take tissues from their cleavages and sleeves which they offer her without saying a word.

When she's calmed down, she gets up on the platform and asks the adjudicator if he'll disqualify the record. He says no, he won't disqualify it. One thing doesn't impinge on the other. They've beaten the record and he's witnessed that. He signs the declaration, hands it over and, even though Bustillo hasn't turned up with his beer, he says he must get a move on, otherwise he'll be late for the paella. But he doesn't move and keeps staring at the mothers.

Hector and Guimaraes have disappeared, and Garriga is afraid they will try to corner the beggars at a cash point and burn them alive (influenced by some video-game). She puts the microphone level with her mouth, in order to read the manifesto. So much rehearsing at home and now it comes out anyhow. She says managers and manageresses don't allow you to breastfeed her, his, your, daughter, son because they don't think it's important. She blows her nose. With only three month's maternity leave they force you to take your child off the tit and this is unfair. In other countries, companies have set up breastfeeding rooms. She clears her throat and calms down a little. Maternal milk prevents children getting lots of illnesses. This is why breastfeeding your daughters and sons is not a sight to be ashamed of. She doesn't know why, but she ends up talking about the importance of fruit-collecting in primitive societies and how, in contrast, only hunting was valued because that's the province of the hominoids, of the male gender. She calls for the adoption of non-sexist terms 'Neanderthal person' and 'Cromagnon person' instead of the sexist 'Neanderthal man' and 'Cromagnon man'. She mentions some prehistoric Venuses. And it's a no show from the telly people.

The Advantages of
Organised Travel

The two daughters secretly save up and give the Figuerolas a week's holiday in Tunisia because it's where they went for their honeymoon twenty-five years ago. They won't stay in the same hotel because it no longer exists. But they have found them one in the same area. Going to Tunisia then wasn't like it is now. Now everybody goes. Before nobody did. It was different before.

The Figuerolas try to pretend they're looking forward to it. They kiss the girls – they still call them 'the girls', though they're nineteen and twenty-three – and ask whose idea it was. The idea came from the Gols, a married couple they see a lot. Mrs Figuerola is thinking she won't last the full seven days with her husband. Her husband is worrying about when he'll be able to masturbate, if she's there all the time.

They both go to pick up the tickets, so as not to upset their daughters. It's Saturday morning and they have a long wait because the agency is packed. They leaf through brochures until it's their turn. A song blasts out from the loudspeakers that Mrs Figuerola always thought was very optimistic: 'Losing my Religion' by REM. She hums it. The song makes her feel like running and playing the lead in video-clips of people hugging.

The sales assistant who's seeing to them brings up the file with their reservation and starts on her sales talk. Her nimble ring finger hits the key of a telephone number programmed straight to central reservations, and when they answer, she asks the odd thing about the package and the travel arrangements. She circles the prices and puts crosses next to the names of the hotels. Everything she does has a neat air, especially the studied way she holds her pen between her index and middle fingers rather than between her index, middle fingers and thumb. Mrs Figuerola thinks she does this because she's got long nails. She remembers that when she went to school she sat at a desk with a girl who was repeating a year, Pili Cabot Duran, who was always asking her: 'Do you want me to tidy your pencil-box?' It was a two-tier box you zipped open and shut. Her coloured pencils were at the bottom and her pens, rulers and sharpeners at the top. First of all, Pili Cabot Duran removed the fingerprints. Then she sharpened the pencils and sequenced them from light to very dark. The young Figuerola went all goose-pimply when she saw her do this, and it's exactly the same now when someone wraps up presents or performs office routines with so much finesse.

They leave when it's coming up to lunchtime. And as they don't want to go home and prepare whatever for just the two of them – the girls are out on their own – they decide to go to the Chinese, where it's not great but at least they give you a tablecloth. Mrs Figuerola is holding various brochures. They'd have preferred New York or London (even if it meant paying a premium).

'What a drag, Tunis, I ask you,' she whinges. And opens the restaurant door. She asks: 'Which table do you want?'

'I don't mind.'

'Yes, you do mind. You choose, because if I choose you'll say I made the wrong choice.'

He chooses the table that's nearest.

They order menu B, but don't crack any jokes about the meat being so cheap because it's the dead ancestors of the Chinese. They only crack jokes when they're with someone else. After a long silence, he says the luxury aspect of Tunis hotels is fake but, nevertheless, the architects there design them that way because they take bad taste for granted.

'Hey, you're a real racist when you turn your mind to it,' she protests.

There's a daily paper on the bar. If there'd been two, it wouldn't have mattered, each could have had one, but as there's only one, will it be hers or will it be his? Both covet it.

'I suppose the hotel has a gym?' he asks.

'So what if it has?' she reacts. 'Are you really likely to go? You make me laugh, you really do. We'll be lucky if there's a toilet en suite.'

He looks down.

The day they travel they squabble over their suitcases just before getting on the plane. She wants them plastic-wrapped so they don't get dirty, and he doesn't see the point. They scowl at each other while they check in. A group of seven or eight in the lobby are waving 'Welcome, Igor' posters. They're wearing T-shirts emblazoned with a boy's face. Adoptive parents waiting it seems.

They don't say a word until they're in their seats on the plane and the hostesses bring the lunch trays. She spreads all her butter on her roll, but leaves a chunk of gruyère that looks like an eraser. He asks her if she'll swap her cheese for his butter – butter always repeats on him. She swaps.

'Welcome to the Third World,' he mutters in the queue to get their passports stamped. She's energised by the fact it's all so haphazard. It's something to talk about when they get back.

'You could smuggle any amount of drugs here. There's no control at all.'

He doesn't really agree, but nods in relief, because he can see she's in a better temper, and thank God for that, given the long evening ahead: no opportunity to kill time watching television or reading, as they do at home, or do anything apart from walk around until it's bedtime. They collect their suitcases that are dirty because in the end they didn't plastic-wrap, and spot their name, Figuerola, mispelt on a card held up by the guide from the travel agency. It says *Figola*. There are other names underneath: Pérez and Ibiriku. She goes over to the guide and identifies herself. Afterwards she whispers to her husband: 'What a drag, my God, waiting for these other couples.'

'Organised travel is horrific,' he agrees. At least, if they're upset by the same things, they can present a united front.

'These people, who can't leave home unless they go in a crowd… can't do things for themselves.'

The missing couples come. One couple look like students the same age as their own daughters. The other two married not long ago. Mrs Figuerola spots that straight away. She's pregnant.

They get into the minibus. Mr Figuerola fetches up next to the girl student and their legs rub against each other. She's very ordinary. The pores on her nose are very dilated and she's on the plump side, but unappetisingly so. He prefers the other woman, so when the one with pores asks her young man to change places, he's delighted. Seated next to the driver, the husband of the one he fancies is reading out the names of the cities advertised on the roadside hoardings, but gets them wrong on purpose. He says Mohammed instead of Hammammet. They're quite infantile jokes, thinks Mr Figuerola, it's the first joke that would occur to a young kid who'd read Hammammet. He laughs. Mrs Figuerola, on the other hand, looks contemptuous.

At the hotel they're shown to a kind of private room and given glasses, rims coated in pink sugar and full of a blue concoction. They take a sip and put the glasses down; it's very sweet and non-alcoholic. Were they given cocktails in the other hotel twenty-five years ago? Bet they drank them. It can't have given them headaches. They call to the bellboy to carry their suitcases up. It's a waste of time sitting there.

'I bet you anything he's never ever got a tip like the one he'll get now,' says Mr Figuerola while they wait for the lift.

'Can't you try to be less classist for three minutes?' she asks, at her wit's end. 'Just three minutes without being so shitty, please?'

They go into their bedroom and look aghast at the bed. The pink counterpane is folded in the shape of a flower. On top is a basket of fruit and a bottle of champagne in an ice-bucket. Italian champagne, they reckon.

'The girls,' he says.

'I'll give them a ring now,' she rasps. And looks for mobile numbers for five or six minutes and makes calls in vain that lead her on to make other calls. 'Àurea? Hello, darling.' She's obviously answering questions with a double meaning. 'Oh of course we'll use them, oh, I don't know, I don't know, I can't say I won't, you know what it's like.'

And yes, she thinks once she's hung up, perhaps it *is* about going to bed with her husband, but is that why she's travelled so far? To go to bed with her husband? They never do unless something quite extraordinary happens, and now they don't ever get lovey-dovey or openly ask for it. They like doing other things now. Cultivating the plants in their second home, buying fertiliser from the Garden Shop, reading, watching the girls grow up, and going on gastronomic tours with the Gols. This is perhaps what they prefer: buying tickets for wine-tastings and going for gourmet meals. He rips the cellophane over the basket. Pineapples and bananas. But they don't feel like pineapple and banana. If only there were some cheese, chocolate or crisps.

'It made sense to give fruit when it was scarce but not now, it's just an old custom that dies hard,' says she. 'It's absurd, totally absurd. It's absurd. An absurdity.'

'What about the champagne – do or don't we open it?' he asks. 'I think it will be quite ghastly.'

'It's a present from your daughters, it's your business, when you go back to Barcelona you can say you didn't like the look of it, that if it's not French champagne, you…' And she takes her fan out of her bag and starts fanning herself.

'Ah…!' he sighs wearily. He cuts the pineapple with the knife that's in the basket and sees it's past its best. He takes the foil wrap off the top of the bottle and starts to twist the wire that's round the plastic cork. What glasses are they going to use, the ones in the bathroom? If they were in love they might, naturally, but in their situation, what are they supposed to do?

'If only there was a mini-bar, at least…' she whinges, because they take turns with the baton when it's time to express annoyance. First one, then the other.

Mrs Figuerola unhooks the phone from where she's lying on the bed and dials 9. She tries to explain herself to the receptionist. Are there any glasses? Yes, there are. Can they send some up? She doesn't know how to say that correctly and the receptionist makes her repeat herself. She taps the receiver and gesticulates at her husband until he takes the phone.

'Ask if they've got crisps, or something savoury?'

Once he's hung up, Mr Figuerola switches on the television and starts flicking. A weatherman is showing a map of Tunisia dotted with suns:

'Look, it's Tunis's answer to Jordi Potau.'

But she doesn't find that funny at all. She's thinking about all the couples that have been to that hotel, seen the weatherman and compared him to the one on the telly at home. She amuses herself by breaking up the carnation-shaped folds of the counterpane and thinking about Pili Cabot Duran. He asks her what she wants to do that evening.

She doesn't reply. She gets up when someone rings. She

picks up his wallet and searches inside.

'Is this a lot or little?' she asks, brandishing a five-dinar note.

'You know, it depends how you look at it.'

'Xevi, they're waiting, right?'

When she opens the door, she finds the same bellboy as before clutching two glasses in one hand – she'd imagined he'd bring them on a trolley – and a small plate, covered by a napkin, in the other. She hands over the note, says goodbye and lifts up the napkin. There are sweet tit-bits. Her eyes glint and a tear runs down her cheek. Recently she's been crying over everything.

They pour the champagne into the tulip-shaped glasses made of thick green glass, as if for ice cream. They don't toast. They only do that if they're with someone else.

He takes a gulp, doesn't know where to look and represses a scowl of horror. They could have been in a good hotel. One with a masseuse, for example. The mere thought turns him on. He must get himself a lover somehow. He's the only one at work who doesn't have one. He can't go on like this; he needs a lover to give him some *joie de vivre*. If he had one, he could be texting her right now, on the quiet. He'd buy her a small present and tell his wife it was for the gang at the office. It would be a young woman who was usually smiling and always wore risqué lingerie. Not so much to ask for, was it? Didn't have to be that pretty or svelte. Before he was too old, he could afford a few restaurant meals and drinks in hotel bars for a girl who looked forward to seeing him, couldn't he?

Mrs Figuerola goes to the toilet. The cellulite on her arms shows up much more in this mirror than in the one at home. She finds one very long, big hair on her shoulder. It's one of those white hairs that crop up in strange places. And she's not brought her tweezers. She tries to pull it out but can't. She looks at her watch and fantasises about what life would be like if she were separated, like her colleagues at work. She'd live in a single woman's flat and the girls would come to see her and stay over. She'd become a writer. Naturally she'd like to go to bed with men, but it's a bit late for that now. She takes her tights and knickers off at the same time, and sits on the bowl. She puts her chin on her knees and goes after the big hair with her fingertips. But doesn't find it. She looks at the floor. Scratches a spot and can't rest till it bursts. On her own, going to work, inviting colleagues from work to dinner, renting films, owning willow-wood shelves. She takes some toilet paper and wipes.

'You had a shit?' he asks her when he sees her come out.

'No, I tried but couldn't. Did you?'

'No, I couldn't either, just wondered whether you had.'

'It's the journey; it's all bunged up. You'll see tomorrow.' And she touches the area again where she thinks that hair is.

He breathes. He always feels relieved if he knows his wife hasn't done it either. He smiles. She shakes her head and clicks her tongue. It would be rather forced for them to hug, if not out of place, but that smile will do her.

More Advantages of Organised Travel

Marc gives Carla the present of a trip to Tunisia to celebrate the fact they're an item again. They buried the hatchet three weeks ago, during the PhiloBang, the Philosophy Faculty Party. Since they started going out together, two years ago, they've split up twice, but have never been separated for as long as now.

They agree to meet at the metro station and go to the travel agency together. He gets there first (she's always late) and sits waiting by the rail. Carla appears round the corner, palms clasped as if in prayer, begging forgiveness.

'Don't kill me! Boring idiots started calling just as I was leaving,' she apologises.

They start walking but don't hold hands. Now they're an item once more, she says she doesn't want to walk along the street as if she were an accessory.

It's Saturday morning and they have a long wait, because the place is full. They leaf through catalogues till it's their turn. An old song blasts out from the loudspeakers that Carla's always thought sad and desperate: 'Losing my Religion'. She can't remember the group's name.

'I'd have preferred something a little more *adventuresome*,' she whinges, yet again.

But the sales assistant who's seeing to them brings up the file with their reservation and starts on her sales talk. Her nimble ring finger hits the key for a telephone number programmed straight to central reservations, and when they answer, she asks the odd thing about the package and travel arrangements. She circles prices and puts crosses next to the names of the hotels. Everything she does has a neat air, especially the studied way she holds her pen between her index and middle fingers rather than between her index, middle fingers and thumb. Carla thinks she does this because she's got long nails.

They leave with the tickets they've purchased (Marc has them) and she suggests going for a coffee 'to discuss their latest trick.' They leaf through the stiff, shiny brochure on a bar terrace, so shiny it reflects their enraptured faces. Marc looks at Carla without her noticing.

'For what we're paying, think we'll get a luxury hotel,' he ruminates, looking forward to it. 'For the same price we'd get a bed and breakfast here.' They can never go to that kind of hotel. They never have.

But she gets angry: she thinks it's rather unfair.

'I think it's rather unfair. Perhaps you chose the wrong course and your real vocation is to do economics.'

As far as Carla is concerned, 'to do economics' is equivalent to becoming part of the capitalist system and surrendering to consumer society, so Marc quickly changes the topic of conversation, because he's scared stiff of disappointing her. He talks about Tunisian cuisine that uses lots of seasonal vegetables and will be just right for their diet and the gymnasium in their hotel, the Hammammet Serail. They don't know what the Serail means. Hammammet, they do; it's a city.

The day they catch their plane they squabble because he reckons they've so little luggage, they don't need to check it in and she thinks they should. They've not squabbled much so far and don't know how to make up quickly and not leave an aftertaste. She looks into space and doesn't answer his questions. When it's time to board they half make up –

declare a tense truce – and it's a shame, because they'd imagined they'd have a very romantic time at the airport (both are wearing new clothes).

Carla goes all miserable for a quarter of the two-hour flight. She daydreams looking out of the window: if the plane were to crash now – and she die – he'd be left feeling remorseful because he'd not loved her enough in her last few minutes of life. Clearly, in the long term, he'd forget her. He'd start going out with Laia again, naturally. The mere thought brings tears to her eyes. Marc acts as if he's offended and as a result can't read the paper. They forgive each other when lunch is served, because it wouldn't be right to eat before they'd made up. He eats the peanuts even though they must be fattening. She gets annoyed: he's got no willpower.

'Welcome to the Third World!' he declares jokingly when they have to queue at passport control. She perks up when she sees it's all so tatty. It's something to talk about on their return.

'You could smuggle any amount of drugs through here. There's no control at all.'

He doesn't really agree, but nods in relief because he sees she's in a better temper, and thank God for that, given the long evening ahead, and no opportunity to kill time watching television or reading, like at home, or do anything apart from walk round until it's bedtime.

They collect their bags – sports gear – from the belt – they did check them in after all – and by the exit see the man from the agency, with a blackboard where her surname is misspelt (why must they always put the man's surname? opines Marc). One couple is still to come.

'*Français*?' asks Carla, emphatically, gesticulating as if she's drowning in a river. '*Vous parlez…?*'

Marc scolds her, half amused, half cocksure. '*Everyone* here speaks French, darling.'

'No need to tell me,' and she gets angry again with him

and his self-importance.

Marc greets the guide and the man and woman waiting there. He whispers and averts his gaze: he's embarrassed about speaking another language. His embarrassment also makes him pronounce it much worse than he needs to. She – who doesn't know French, she studied English at university – asks him what he's said. But the missing couple turns up when he was about to reply he'd said nothing really.

'So the whole herd's ready,' Carla whinges. He doesn't respond. It was a struggle to persuade her to go on a package (think it will be a laugh, we'll see how people go to Tunis and don't budge from the hotel swimming pool, we'll get all the benefits and none of the disadvantages). The newcomers greet them shyly. One of the couples is young and the girl is pregnant. The others are as old as Carla's parents. Marc's are not so old.

Once in the minibus she notices the old man's leg rubbing against hers. It's impossible for legs not to touch because there's no room at all but even so she tries to make Marc jealous by ensuring he registers that the stranger fancies her.

'Can we change seats?' she whispers, 'Granddad is getting the hots for me.'

He believes her and hurriedly complies. He scrutinises the man for the whole journey, and whatever he does – look out the window, not look at Carla – seems like a sign of guilt. Days of torture lie ahead, he knows, with such a sexpot, desirable girlfriend in an Arab country. He should have gone for Greece, that was also on special offer. But he doesn't say as much to her or she'll think he's racist.

The husband of the pregnant lady, who's sitting next to the driver, has plucked up courage and is reading the names of the cities out loud, but getting them in the wrong order to raise a laugh. He says Mohammed instead of Hammammet. Carla suffers on behalf of driver and guide.

'They don't know how to behave away from home,' she

mutters in Marc's ear. 'They can't handle difference.'

Then he spots an amusing name and can't prevent himself from saying it aloud. The others cheer and clap.

They all get off at the first stop except for the expectant couple who are going to another hotel. It's obvious they're worried they've got a worse hotel than this one. Carla and Marc, on the other hand, smile optimistically, because the Hammammet Serail seems well set up. It's full of Arab fountains and tiles.

'*Bonsoir*,' he greets the bellboy who comes out to welcome them. The man takes their bags, bows his head and tells them there's a complimentary drink.

'What did *he* want?' she asks. But her boyfriend doesn't need to explain, because the man accompanies them to a kind of private room with a low polygonal table. They sit on dark blue velvet cushions. She runs a jagged nail (she chews them) and draws a kind of trail over one that turns lighter in colour. She erases it with the palm of her hand and it disappears. She amuses herself like that until they bring their glasses, rims coated in pink sugar, and full of a blue concoction.

'Are you going to try it? It's a complimentary welcome cocktail,' says Marc.

They sip voraciously. Their resolve to keep to their diet wavers. Carla gets very impatient when he's still not finished.

She leaves her ID card at reception but the bellboy wants both. He takes a map and their key. Another couple comes and leaves their key. The woman's wet hair is combed back, and a small camera is dangling from her wrist. She waves to the bellboy to come over and tries to ask him about places to go for dinner, but makes no headway. She doesn't speak French.

'So why didn't you help her?' Carla asks. She means like

an interpreter. If she knew the language, she'd not think twice. She'd like to do that.

'I don't know,' he replies, wearily but complacently. And then he adopts the ironic tone he always uses when they're travelling, because he feels superior when they're on their travels. Outside her natural space, she, in contrast, turns more dull-witted. 'There'll be time enough for that.'

'It's incredible how people who don't know a language start shouting because they think that's the way to be understood,' says Carla.

He agrees.

They go into their bedroom and Marc makes a beeline for the toilet. In the meantime, Carla pushes together the two beds, that are very light, to make a double bed. She re-positions the bedside tables. Then takes the coasters they were given on the plane from the pages of the book she is reading. She tries to act upbeat.

'For our album!' she exclaims.

One of her duties as the female member of the couple is to do the album. She has to keep cinema tickets, napkins with little drawings and plaques from champagne corks (but only from the bottles they've drunk), packets of sugar from bars where they've made up and ID bracelets from music festivals where they've kissed. She opens the travel bag and takes out her change of clothes. She hangs it up in the wardrobe.

'Poppet!' she shouts, because she's suddenly noticed some plates on the desk, covered in film-wrap. 'They've left dinner for us.'

'Really?' He looks round.

'Shall we eat it?'

Marc shrugs his shoulders. If he says he feels hungry, she'll perhaps get angry: it's cold meats and bread. The meats make you fat and the bread isn't wholemeal. To avoid committing himself, he switches the telly on and starts flicking. A weatherman is pointing to a map of Tunisia full of suns.

'Look, it's Mohammed Potau,' he jokes. And she starts to laugh, and he feels pleased that worked.

'Is there a porno channel in this hotel?' she asks.

He steers clear of answering that one. When he first met her he thought she was a very liberal-minded girl. She was always talking about pornography as if she really liked it. He now knows she only does it to look trendy, and if he dared look at the pornography channel for the free minute, she'd go home a deeply jealous woman.

'You going to have a shower?' she also asks.

'Possibly not.'

'I am. I feel all sweaty.'

'But don't you want to have dinner first?'

'That depends. Are we going out after, or not?'

Marc looks though the window. He'd imagined the hotel would be in the centre of Tunis. That you'd step out of the hotel and see cafés with fans in the ceiling and lots of men sitting on carpets smoking water pipes. But they're in an area full of whitewashed blocks that remind him of the outskirts of Palma. They'll have to get a taxi to go to the centre, and he's afraid they'll get swindled or it will be very expensive (he's paying for the trip and the budget's tight). But he doesn't feel like staying there till it's time to go sleep, because it's still early. Obviously he could make a sexual advance. If she responds, that might at best take a good hour, then it would be time for dinner, and would be a decent time to go to sleep. And tomorrow they could get up early to make the most of the day. Now, if he had the choice, he'd read the newspapers they were given on the flight. But she hates him reading the newspapers. She likes to buy and have them but just the sight of him skimming the headlines makes her scowl. Marc imagines it must be a female trait, because the Laia he went out with when he broke off with Carla acted likewise. She'd be desperate to go to the terrace of a bar 'to read the paper' but, when he started to, she'd complain she felt like a piece of the furniture.

Anyway it was not a good idea to make a sexual advance. If he starts mauling her, she'll suspect he doesn't want to spend money on a taxi. He'll deny it but she won't believe him. They'll argue. Finally, he'll apologise and she'll say she doesn't intend getting into another taxi ever. She'll stick to her guns for the whole of their stay in Tunis and they'll be forced to travel on buses all the time. When he tries to say, 'Come on, poppet, get in the taxi, darling,' she'll run off in a huff, and he'll have to chase after her to ensure she doesn't get raped.

'We could eat this and then call a taxi and go for a walk round the centre,' Marc suggests (he'll always have time to read the paper, and perhaps try a sexual advance, after their stroll).

'It's not low calorie,' complains Carla. In non-dieting mood, she feels more like a pizza than that sort of sliced meat.

'If you like we'll pass on dinner and have tea with Arab pastries. Tea and pastries must be worth four hundred calories.'

She loves his suggestion. She also imagines a bar with a ceiling fan and mosquito nets. They change as they look at television channels and comment on the beautiful – quite 70s they reckon – news presenter, and the difference between the weatherman on their television (Potau) and this other weatherman.

When they leave the hotel they see a long row of taxis waiting. They take one and she tells the driver in her gibberish to take them to the centre, but the man doesn't understand a word. Marc gets the map out and tells him the name of an avenue, trying not to offend her because he might be undermining her authority. He studied it in the toilet while she was making herself up in the mirror in the hallway. She doesn't normally make herself up but does when they're travelling, in order to look good in their photos.

'Fuck. I left the camera in the hotel,' says Marc. She doesn't lose her temper.

Luckily he doesn't overcharge, or drive them to the outskirts and rob them, or any of the terrible things he imagines can happen in a place like Tunis. They get out of the taxi and, immediately, two or three men offer them fish-shaped earrings; the typical fish that bring good luck. She acts as if she's expert at bartering. He's happy to let her get on with it. He can't stand it and is no good at it.

'If we buy some, the other sellers will leave us in peace,' Carla pontificates.

He looks at her bartering as if her life depended on it. And for a moment it seems she's right but other men are always popping up with their own sets of fishy earrings. A man bows before them and says he'll take them to a kind of museum, a young kid begs, and all of a sudden it gets tiresome. They are fed up with so many people around them as they walk. Marc feels angry. If he had some fly spray he'd exterminate the lot. They make gradual progress while the motley retinue continues behind them and he's pained by her harsh tone when she shouts she doesn't want anything.

They sit at a table in a bar. It's not the bar they'd imagined (no mosquito nets or pipe-smokers), but, at least, there are other foreigners, also up to here with the place. They order mint tea and pastries and when the waiter brings them, Carla complains bad-temperedly they're much more than four hundred calories, and jam-filled. And they're not homemade but mass-produced.

For two or three minutes they find looking at their new surroundings quite entertaining. There's a man holding a half-bald, stooping camel by the bit. It's in case anyone wants to take photos. A shoeshiner who also sells fishy earrings comes over to Marc. He asks him how many camels he wants for Carla. He says she's not for sale, both terrified and flattered.

'Poppet! This guy wants to buy you!'

The man persists, Forty-five camels? Marc refuses again smiling to show he understands – but doesn't share – the traditions of others. A hundred? No. Two hundred?

Carla herself pompously warns him off: '*Féministe. Je suis féministe.*' And then, as he doesn't look at all enlightened. She asks Marc: 'Did I say it properly? Tell him I'm not your property, that if he wants something he must ask me.'

'No, or we'll never get rid of him.'

Her man repeats the word *féministe* as if it was a solid reason to forget the idea of purchasing her. But he comes back at him. He outlines her shape with his hands to show he thinks she's pretty. Two hundred and fifty camels. No, no and no again, for fuck's sake.

After this cut and thrust, the man gestures despondently, as if surrendering, and shows them earrings. She's amused and asks him how much he wants, barters and finally buys them. The man seems so annoyed he couldn't take her to his harem that he grabs her money almost reluctantly.

'That was really heavy,' says Carla when they're by themselves. This is something to talk about when we get back. Do you know they wanted to buy my girlfriend for two hundred and fifty camels? God, Marc, why didn't you sell her? Because I didn't want to inflict her on the Arab world. She kisses him noisily. In the evening, when they go to bed, she'll tell him he's in a harem and that all the sheiks desire her, but she will only be his. 'Thanks for not selling me.' And she smiles and acts up sexily.

Marc gives her a hug. He's happy as well and tonight he'll tell her he's paid two hundred and fifty camels for her, and she's his sexual slave. She's got to do everything to pleasure him (maybe, even agree to a blow-job).

'You know, if he'd gone to three hundred camels, I'd have sold you.'

She squeezes his arm playfully.

'Back in a minute,' she replies. 'You want another tea?'

'Yes, but take care.' He knows she's really going to the toilet. She's too embarrassed to go in the hotel bedroom.

And he watches her walk in the bar, swaying her bum. She's really happy, more than happy now. The shoeshiner is by the table furthest down the street, the one in front of a couple who look like German pensioners. He's offering a hundred camels for the wife who's incredibly ugly and the irritated husband is waving his hand to get him to move on. Marc who'd really believed the man wanted to buy his Carla, never imagined it was a trick to sell their goods, and he looks at the scene, half aggrieved, half relieved, until she gets back.

The Silence Room

SEAN O'BRIEN

ISBN: 978 1905583171
RRP: £7.95

'Sean O'Brien does for libraries what Ursula Andress did for bikinis. Read and rejoice!' - Val McDermid

Chain-smoking alcoholics, warring academics, gothic stalkers and aspiring writers are just some of the visitors that browse the mysterious library at the heart of Sean O'Brien's fiction debut. Idlers and idolisers alike can be referenced, in body or in text, among the crepuscular alcoves and dim staircases of this seemingly unassuming building. The secret to a family curse, a dog-eared first edition of Stevens' Harmonium, the gruesome fate of a feminist literary theorist - all are available to simply take down from the shelf, as are the catalogue of genres and subject areas that O'Brien himself effortlessly deploys: from gothic horror to English pastoral, Critical Theory to Cold War noir.

'Sean O'Brien, like Graham Greene, creates his own instantly recognisable fictional landscape, where crime, mystery and disillusion lurk by the waters of the Tyne or Humber. His stories glint with black comedy and touches of the macabre and surreal. In O'Brien country you may hear the hoot of a train pulling out of the city, but you'll never be on it, because your place is here in the kingdom of backstreet pubs, tired, desirable girls and drowned men. Nothing is ever as it seems: it is much more frightening than that... First-class stories from one of our finest writers.' - Helen Dunmore

Under the Dam
and other stories

DAVID CONSTANTINE

ISBN: 0954828011
RRP: £7.95

'Flawless and unsettling'
Boyd Tonkin, Books of the Year, *The Independent*

'I started reading these stories quietly, and then became obsessed, read them all fast, and started re-reading them again and again. They are gripping tales, but what is startling is the quality of the writing. Every sentence is both unpredictable and exactly what it should be. Reading them is a series of short shocks of (agreeably envious) pleasure.'
- A S Byatt, Book of the Week, *The Guardian*

'A superb collection'- *The Independent*

'This is a haunting collection filled with delicate clarity. Constantine has a sure grasp of the fear and fragility within his characters.'
- A L Kennedy